Guardians of the Dark

Simon Says

BIANCA D'ARC

This book is a work of fiction. The names, characters, places, and incidents are products of the writer's imagination or have been used fictitiously and are not to be construed as real. Any resemblance to persons, living or dead, actual events, locale or organizations is entirely coincidental.

No part of this book may be used or reproduced in any manner whatsoever without written permission, except in the case of brief quotations embodied in critical articles and reviews.

1st Edition
Copyright © 2010 Bianca D'Arc
Published by Kensington Publishing, Inc.

2nd Edition
Copyright © 2019 Bianca D'Arc
Published by Hawk Publishing, LLC

Copyright © 2019 Bianca D'Arc

All rights reserved.

ISBN-13: 978-1-950196-04-3

Special Forces soldier Simon Blackwell ended his affair with Mariana Daniels a while ago, but he hasn't stopped protecting her. Mariana has no knowledge of the dark, deadly creatures that lurk in the forest surrounding her clinic, or of the mysterious powers that make Simon the only one who can defeat them. But soon he'll have no choice but to reveal the truth, and urge her to trust in an explosive passion that never faded…

AUTHOR'S NOTE & DEDICATION

Note: This is the second edition of this story, which first appeared as part of a two-book set titled ***Half Past Dead*** which also featured a story by the talented Zoe Archer. I enjoyed working with her on the set and remain friendly with her to this day. However, the set has run its course, as such things do, and I'm pleased to now be able to release this story on its own as the introduction to my ***Guardians of the Dark*** series.

It was written in June of 2009, when my life was about as happy as it's ever been. I was traveling for a family reunion and was so glad to have all of us in one place…for the last time. Not long after I turned this story in, we learned my mother had cancer and we would never have another chance for us all to be together like that.

I was in such a state at the time that I didn't even include a dedication in the first edition. I'd like to rectify that now and just dedicate this to the memory of my beloved mother, who was incredibly supportive of my radical career change to full-time writing. She never really got to see it all come to fruition, but I'm comforted that she at least knew about the contracts for this series and saw it as a stepping stone on my way to future success.

As with most things in life, it didn't work out quite like we thought it would in 2009, but it *did* work out—probably due to my sweet Guardian Angel who now watches over me from above, as she can no longer guide me here on Earth. I miss you, Mom.

PROLOGUE

"Bravo one. Echo delta niner." Simon repeated the prearranged code for extraction. His small team was mostly gone, decimated by an enemy for which they'd had no adequate way to prepare. They'd been briefed, but nothing could match encountering the walking dead for real for the first time.

"Sitrep," someone barked over the radio. He knew that voice. It was Matt Sykes, an old friend, comrade in arms, and the officer in charge of this little fiasco.

"Jenkins and Bradley are dead. Hsu has gone over to the dark side. Wally and me are the only ones left." That was more than enough reason to get the hell out of Dodge.

Simon wasn't about to mention his own injury. The eggheads on base said one bite from the creatures they were hunting brought instant death. Simon had been lucky so far. He'd been scratched up by their claws, but not bitten. The claws were probably harmless as far as spreading the contagion went. Maybe they had to get a good hard bite out of you in order to spread their infection.

That was something the doctors could puzzle out later. Right now, Simon needed to get himself and Wally out of the hot zone so they could regroup and come back stronger with reinforcements. Lots of reinforcements.

"A helo is coming to get you. ETA ten minutes. Hang tight, Si." Matt's voice was reassuring but Simon caught sight of movement in the trees.

They had to get to the rendezvous, but they were being pursued. They could move faster than their pursuers, but the creatures had the advantage of numbers. If they managed to box him and Wally in, they'd be toast. Or rather, a tasty snack for these ghouls who liked to eat human flesh.

"We're on the move," Simon reported. "Being pursued. Tell the helo to come in hot and be ready to fly. We'll most likely have company on our six. We won't have time to stop and chat."

"Simon…" Matt sounded ready to read him the riot act, but Simon didn't have time to listen. The enemy had found them. He could see the creatures maneuvering through the trees to flank them.

"Gotta go, commander. We'll be at the LZ in ten. Blackwell out."

Wally, otherwise known as Ensign Rob Wallace, the newest member of the team, came crashing through the underbrush. So much for stealth.

"They're flanking us. Bradley and Jenkins are with them."

"Shit." Their former teammates had risen from the dead and were now playing for the other team. Could this day get any worse?

They'd been sent into a horror movie with inadequate intel, inappropriate weaponry and not a chance in hell of winning. Bullets didn't stop these things. They were already dead. Nothing short of a block of well-placed C4 that could blow the bastards to smithereens would stop them. Simon had lost three friends already to this menace, not to mention the Marines that had been sent in before they'd called Special Forces.

"Stay with me, Wally." Simon could see fear in the young man's eyes. "Helo's coming. We just need to keep it together until they get here. I don't want to enter the LZ until the last minute. Otherwise, we'll be forced to make a stand in the clearing or fall back. Neither one of those things is an option." Simon talked fast as he moved with Wally to a better position. "We don't stand a chance if we try to take them on head to head. The ammo we have doesn't work against them. The only thing that seems to do any good are grenades, but they have to be close enough to blow them apart. Just hitting them with shrapnel won't stop them, so use your remaining grenades sparingly. How many you got left?"

Wally did a quick check of his utility belt. "Just one, sir."

"Better than me. I'm out." They'd each been issued five grenades back at base before this mission. When they'd set out on this journey, it had seemed like more than enough to take down a few tangos in the woods. Now Simon knew differently. A whole crate of grenades might not be sufficient to take out these nightmare creatures.

Simon held up one hand for silence. He listened hard to the surrounding forest. All the wildlife had long since vanished. Critters knew better than to stick around when there was a predator in the area. The leaves rustled as the undead moved through the forest, brushing against the foliage.

"They're on the move. We need to go." Simon stood. Wally followed behind. "We have five minutes to kill before the helo gets to the clearing."

Near as Simon could tell, the walking dead no longer comprehended language. They could still hear though, and small sounds would give away Simon and Wally's location. Simon whispered, keeping his voice as low as possible.

The creatures seemed to retain some of the training they'd had in life. They were good at stealth for one thing. The Marines were good at moving silently when they chose. The members of Simon's team who had been lost to the enemy, only to rise from the dead, were even better.

Maybe that's why Simon fell into their trap. One minute he was making plans with Wally under cover of a big maple tree, the next, claws ripped into his shoulder and teeth sank into his flesh.

The fucker had bitten him!

Wally kicked the creature away from Simon, but not in time. Blood welled and Simon knew he'd fall fast if the deaths of his teammates were anything to go by.

Still, the instinct for self-preservation pushed him onward. He ran alongside Wally to the circle of trees that marked the clearing. The helicopter would land in a few minutes but Simon would probably be dead by then.

He'd seen Hsu drop about twenty seconds after he'd been bitten, and beefy Beau Bradley had taken only ten seconds more than that. The poison would course through his body, felling him like one of the mighty trees in this idyllic forest turned horror movie set. Any second now.

Creatures surrounded them. They were coming across the clearing and up from behind. Not much chance of escape from this mess now, and Simon was already dead.

"Get out of here, Wally. I'm done. Save yourself."

At that precise moment, they both heard the sound of helicopter blades in the distance, growing closer.

"Get into the clearing," Simon ordered the younger man. "Use the grenade if you have to. Your ride's almost here."

"I'm not going without you, sir." Wally pointed toward the line of undead Marines standing between them and the Landing Zone. "Ain't no way I'm getting through that line alone."

Simon shook his head and started forward. "I'll take 'em down if I can. You run for the chopper."

Wally nodded his agreement. Both of them knew Simon was living on borrowed time. The least he could do was get young Wally to safety before his time ran out.

"Tell Matt Sykes I'll see him in hell." Simon grinned, thinking of his old comrade and the good friends he'd lost along the way.

"It's been an honor serving with you, sir." Wally spared Simon one long look before they both turned to face the enemy.

They could see the helicopter now. It was coming in for a landing. If they timed it just right, they could make a hole through the mass of creatures for Wally to run through and jump onto the chopper. It was his only shot.

"You know, sir, it's got to have been more than a minute and you're still standing," Wally observed as they waited for the opportune moment to launch their offensive.

Simon stopped breathing for a split second, thinking about what Wally had said. "Yeah, you're right."

"Could be the science guys were wrong. You might live." Wally shrugged but Simon could feel the air vibrate around him as the helicopter came closer. It was almost time. "I think you should come with me, sir." Wally had to shout to be heard above the roar of the helicopter's blades.

"I think you're right, Wallace," Simon shouted back, a grin splitting his face as the helo descended toward the grassy clearing. "We'll both get out of this mess." Almost there. They had to time this right as the monsters tightened the noose around them. "On three. One. Two…" Simon gave a war cry as he ran toward the enemy, hoping like hell that brute force would allow him and Wally to muscle their way past the armada facing them.

He pushed past the first row of stinking flesh easily. The second line was a little harder. He looked over at Wally, but the kid was holding his own. This was like an evil game of football where the stakes were life or death. Simon fought through the secondary line, dodging grasping hands and shouldering through the ranks of dead Marines.

He made it to the open door of the helicopter and looked back to see Wally, in the grip of Lieutenant Hsu. Simon turned to go back and help Wally but hands from inside the chopper grabbed him, tugging him forcefully aboard. He fought against them, but there were too many people gripping him in too many places, pulling him into the hovering helicopter.

The last Simon saw of Wally, he was surrounded by zombies, their teeth ripping into his living flesh. Then Wally pulled the pin on his last remaining grenade.

CHAPTER 1

He watched from the bushes, gauging the woman's reactions as she peered up at the full moon from her back porch. She wasn't wary, and that was a dangerous thing. For her.

Dark things prowled the night. Things out of nightmares. Things a woman like her should never encounter.

If he had his way, she never would. It was his job to see that she remained ignorant of the creatures that stalked the forest behind her home. He was her silent protector, though she would never know it.

If things went as planned...

Hours later, Simon cursed his bad luck. His plan had gone right out the proverbial window, but he was a hell of an improviser. His fast actions and lightning reflexes had saved his life more than once in the past. This time, however, he might've cut things just a little too close. Only the dawn pinkening the eastern sky had saved him tonight, sending the creatures he hunted to ground.

In the night, the hunter had become the hunted and now he was injured. Blood drew the undead creatures like moths to a flame. Simon had left a blood trail through the forest that would have the zombies in a frenzy when they rose again.

Thankfully, the day was sunny and he knew from experience that the reanimated corpses shunned the sun's cleansing rays. They'd be in hiding until sunset. Or until storm clouds showed up. Cloudy days were the worst, because then he had no respite from hunting the creatures that should never have been let loose in the first place.

Simon headed for the deep woods that would take him eventually to Quantico, the Marine base from which he was currently operating. He had been recruited to eradicate the threat in the woods surrounding the base before it could spread any further.

Ostensibly, he was a civilian contractor doing some unspecified work on base. Only a select few high up in the command structure knew his true identity and his real mission. One man against a potential army of the undead wasn't great odds. Simon's training, unique skill set, covert operations experience, and immunity to the contagion that had created these monsters tipped the scales in his favor.

Until today. Today he would be lucky to make it back to base without passing out. He would head straight for the small clinic that served as an infirmary for men in the field. He would go there even though he'd been avoiding that one particular place for weeks now. Not the place really. In truth, it was the woman who worked there he had been trying so hard to avoid. He'd guarded her. He'd watched over her from afar, but he'd been avoiding a face-to-face confrontation with the woman out of his past. The one he'd let get away.

Now, if his rotten luck held, he would be unable to avoid her.

Dr. Mariana Daniels arrived at the base infirmary early, as was her habit. She had only a few more weeks left as a naval officer before she finally returned to civilian life. It had been a long time since she had first put on the uniform. At one time, she had thought to make the military her life's work. Now, over a decade later, she was ready to start a new adventure in the civilian world.

She opened the door to her office and set her coffee cup down on the cluttered desk. A commotion from the front of the clinic made her turn. Usually, she had a good half hour alone before the rest of the staff started reporting for duty in the small infirmary that was just a field branch of the larger medical facility on base. She retraced her steps, curious to see who was early.

She rounded a corner and stopped short in the hall, face to face with a man she'd thought never to see again.

"Simon?" Shock colored her voice.

"Damn."

All this time apart, and the first word out of his mouth was a curse. She shouldn't have expected anything different. Her time with Simon Blackwell had been a low point in her life from which she was still recovering. To be fair, he had also been a high point. Their short-lived relationship had made her happier than she had ever been. Then he'd left with little fanfare. One day he was there, the next he was gone, leaving her to pick up the pieces.

She shouldn't have been surprised. That's what Special Forces guys were like. When they got called up for a mission, they had to leave and couldn't say where they were going or when they would be back. At first she had waited. Only when she'd run into one of his teammates a few months later had she finally realized he wasn't coming back. At least not back to her. He was alive according to his friend, but the prolonged silence where she was concerned told her all she needed to know.

He still looked as handsome as ever, those twinkling blue eyes all too serious and clouded with…pain? She looked him over and realized he was holding his arm abnormally close to his chest and leaving a faint blood trail down the crisp white corridor.

"You're injured."

He nodded, still apparently a man of few words. "I wouldn't have come here otherwise."

Now that hurt. She tried not to flinch, but Simon had always been a little too perceptive.

"I didn't mean it that way, Mari. I figured it would be better for you if you didn't know I was here, on base."

She ushered him into a curtained treatment area and watched as he sat unsteadily on the paper-draped table. She didn't like the pale look of his tanned skin.

"What happened to you?"

"Field exercise. Training accident." His clipped words told her there was a lot more to the story than met the eye. His tone told her not to pry.

She'd known going into their relationship that he was a Special Operations guy. What he'd been doing in the months since she had last seen him was a mystery. Simon Blackwell lived much of his life on a need-to-know basis. It had been hard to deal with while they'd been dating, but she had always understood duty and honor. She had even admired him for his devotion to both.

Mariana stepped closer and started examining his injuries. There were multiple gashes running along one side of his body and some of them looked deep. A few would probably require stitches.

"Well, your field exercise seems to have put you in the path of...are these claw marks?"

"Ran into a badger. Got scratched up."

"Ah, I see. A badger...with what looks like a serrated edged weapon in addition to some very nasty claws."

She gasped as he grabbed her hand, stilling her motions. "Don't push, Mari." His tone was both familiar and forbidding.

Silence passed between them as she regarded him. He had always had an intensity about him that made her want to swoon. A badass vibe that turned her on like nothing else. He had locked eyes with her a couple of times while they were making love and she'd thought she'd seen her future in his bottomless blue gaze.

She'd been wrong.

"All right. I won't ask any more questions. Other than medical questions, of course. You're up to date on your tetanus, right?"

He nodded, letting go of her hand and she relaxed fractionally.

She took a closer look at his wounds. The slashes and claw marks extended over his biceps and onto his chest. The shirt had to go.

He wore a dark green camouflage Battle Dress Uniform shirt. They were called BDUs for short, and the shirt was more properly called a blouse, but that had always sounded a little too feminine to Mariana. It buttoned up the front, which would make it easy to get off him.

With deft movements, she began unbuttoning the heavy-weight cotton shirt. She was surprised when he stilled her hands as she worked her way down his muscled abdomen.

"I'll get the rest."

She nodded tightly and turned to locate the scissors. They were on the instrument tray kept ready in every treatment area. Simon's olive drab undershirt would have to be cut off him. It was torn and tattered already, as was the heavier cotton of the BDU shirt. The undershirt would be easy to cut through to clean and dress his wounds, while the BDU top would be too much for her little scissors.

Turning back to him, scissors in hand, she got her first good look at his physique, clad only in the form-fitting undershirt. It had been months since she had last seen him. Damn, the man still had the power to push the breath from her lungs. He followed her movements with a guarded expression as she drew closer. She tried desperately not to betray the unwanted attraction that still flowed through her body for him.

Simon had always been a bad boy she should have known to stay away from in the first place. Unfortunately for her heart, he was also too compelling to resist. He had never been overly talkative. Of course, when they'd been together, the furthest thing from her mind had been conversation. Theirs had been an explosive passion. Even memories of their time together were enough to get her hot and bothered.

So she tried her best not to think about him. It worked, more now than it had in the beginning. It had gotten so that now she could go whole days without something triggering a memory of their short time as a couple. She'd given her heart to the man, though she'd never said it to him in so many words. She'd been afraid of scaring him off.

Simon had always been the strong, silent type. A man of few words, he was all about action. He had just about ruined her for other men, though he'd never done anything to deliberately hurt her. Except leave and not come back.

She kept reminding herself that they'd made no promises to each other. Mariana had been rudely awakened when he didn't return. She realized then that any emotional attachments in their relationship had been totally on her side. Simon hadn't led her on. She didn't blame him for toying with her affections. She had done the hatchet job on her own heart.

And now, here he was, bleeding and in need of help in her clinic. He still didn't talk much, and she could see a new wariness that hadn't been there before. Those pretty blue eyes were truly the mirrors of his soul. He didn't betray much in his expression, but she had often thought she could tell what was going on in his active brain by watching the subtle nuances in his stunning baby blues.

Maybe that was self-delusion as well.

She shrugged off the thoughts of what had been and what could have been. He held his BDU shirt in one hand. She took it from him and tossed it onto the counter.

"That shirt is ruined."

"I have a few things in the top pockets I'd like to get before we chuck it in the trash."

She turned back to him, armed with her small scissors. "I'll leave it here for now. Let's get you fixed up and then we'll deal with everything else."

"Sounds like a good plan to me."

She went to work on his undershirt, cutting it away a little at a time. The gashes on his arm and chest were deeper than she had originally thought and they got worse the more they were revealed.

"How long ago did this happen?" She was all business now. He had to be in serious pain, but nothing showed on his face.

"About oh-four-hundred."

"And you walked all the way in?" She consulted the clock on the wall. "It took you three hours to get here?" Damn, the man had a will of iron. Any normal guy would have collapsed by now.

"About that." He shrugged his uninjured shoulder as if walking three hours through rough terrain while seriously wounded and dripping blood was no big deal. Perhaps to him, it wasn't. The thought was chilling.

"All right. I'm going to start an IV to replace some of your fluids." She reached for a blood pressure cuff and wrapped it efficiently around his uninjured arm. The slashes and scratches were on his left side, leaving his right arm relatively unscathed. She knew he was right handed, so at least he would have the use of his dominant arm as he healed.

She heard the front door open and the chatter of two of her nurses arriving. Thank goodness. She shouted to get their attention and in short order she had them bustling around Simon. His blood pressure was lower than it should be and she monitored him closely as the IV began to do its work.

Simon lay back on the padded table at a slight incline, watching Mariana as the three women bustled around him. He was out of it. The blood loss had been worse than he had expected. He was so light-headed at this point, it felt like the small treatment room was spinning around him. Luckily, his own personal guardian angel knew what to do. She would save his miserable hide so he could go on protecting her from afar.

The situation was truly fucked up. If he'd had a choice he

would have stayed far away from Mariana. He was no good for her. A guy with his baggage could only drag her down. He'd glimpsed it during their brief affair. He'd seen the way she looked at him, with forever in her eyes, and he knew he couldn't be that guy. He couldn't be the guy who would make her life the fairy tale it was supposed to be.

No, all his fairy tales ended in death. There was no happily ever after in his world. Never had been. And now there never would be. All chance of changing his luck had been taken away on that last mission. The mission that had changed his life and put Mari forever out of his reach.

When duty had called him away from her addictive presence, at first he'd had every intention of returning. Then things had happened—changes had been made to his very being—and he knew he would have to stay away from her. Far away. He had kept tabs on her as best he could, though. He hadn't been able to help himself. And when he'd been tasked with clearing the woods near Quantico, he'd been unable to keep himself from watching her. The woman mesmerized him and made him yearn for things he could no longer have.

Then he'd suffered a moment of miscalculation last night and here he was, lying on a thinly padded examination table while she fussed over him. She touched him with gentle fingers, even while she probed and cleaned the deepest of his wounds. Her warm breath breezed over his skin as she put a few stitches across the worst of the cuts and his gut clenched in reaction. If those nurses hadn't been in the room, he didn't know what he would have done. It was all he could do to control himself when Mariana was this close.

She smelled as good as he remembered. A little hint of gardenia mixed with her own delicate scent. It was intoxicating.

But she wasn't for him. He had to keep reminding himself of that sad fact. He could only screw up her life with the weirdness that had taken over his world. Mariana was better off without the likes of him. Too bad her big brown eyes made him want to forget all his damned good reasons for staying away.

"Almost done," she promised as she went to work on the last of the deep gouges on his chest. Her touch was soft and gentle, but being stitched hurt, regardless of the topical anesthetic she had applied. "How are you feeling?"

"Better." His head was clearing and he noted the way she glanced at her assistants—particularly the nurse who still had his right arm in the blood pressure cuff.

The nurse reported some numbers that sounded markedly better than his last reading and deflated the cuff. Simon clenched his fist a few times to dissipate the tingling sensation in his arm. He found himself unable to look away from Mariana. She was still just as beautiful as she had been when they'd first met. More beautiful, in fact, even though strain showed in the gentle lines of her face. The soft curves of her body still made his mouth water. She had filled out in all the right places.

He knew medical school and residency had taken a lot out of her. She had been just a little too skinny, in his opinion, when they'd first met, years ago. It had taken him time to work up the nerve—and to be in one place long enough—to ask her out. They'd dated, off and on, for just over a year when that last mission sent him on another path completely. But just looking at her now brought it all back. The attraction. The want. The need.

He did his best to suppress any outward display of interest, knowing it probably wouldn't be welcome. He'd left her. He'd hurt her. There was no doubt in his mind that was the case. She was too soft-hearted not to be hurt by his complete lack of communication.

He had taken the coward's way out by not saying goodbye. At the time, it had seemed the best thing to do. He hadn't been sure he would be strong enough to end it if he had to see her again. She was as addictive as any drug. At least to him. Though she probably hadn't known it. Simon had been careful to hide his feelings. He hadn't wanted to lead her on.

"Who's your CO, Si?" She surprised him with the gently voiced question about his commanding officer. His thoughts had drifted so far, he almost jumped when her question brought him back to Earth, but his training held him in check.

"I'm a civilian now, Mari."

She looked at him in surprise as she finished with the last of his stitches. "A contractor? Don't tell me you're working for those black ops guys in the swamp."

He should have known she would jump to the right conclusion. She had a quick mind and a wide knowledge of military and political things one wouldn't necessarily expect of a medical officer.

"You know I can't tell you, Mari. Everything about my presence here is on a need-to-know basis."

"Well, right now I need to know who to report your injury to. You must have a CO on base."

She was right, but he didn't really want her any more involved than she already was. "Give me the phone and I'll report in."

She stared at him for a moment, probably deciding whether to argue, then finally turned toward the wall phone, snatching up the handset. She handed it to him and he sent a pointed look at the two nurses, who were busy with various tasks in the small space.

"Oh, for heaven's sake," she grumbled, sending the two ladies on their way, giving them errands to run in other parts of the infirmary. It wasn't truly private, of course. Still, it was good enough for him to report his location and condition. He wouldn't get into any incriminating details of his mission while on a public phone line anyway. Mariana turned back to him as the other two women bustled off. "What number?"

He couldn't reach the wall mounted keypad from where he sat. He would rather she didn't know who he called, but there was no other choice. He gave her the commander's extension number and a raised eyebrow was her only response. She dialed for him, then turned to leave the enclosure, giving him the illusion of privacy.

Soon after he ended the call, Mari returned, taking the handset and hanging it up for him. He had no doubt she had heard every word of his brief conversation, but no comments on the call were forthcoming. She didn't speak at all, in fact, as she continued to monitor his vital signs and work on the less severe of his wounds. She had taken care of the most serious first. All that were left were a few shallow scratches and bruises.

The silent treatment was driving him nuts. He knew he owed her an apology at the very least, for the way he had ended their relationship. He had never been the most eloquent of men and still didn't know how to make her understand his reasoning. A bare bones apology would have to do. It was a good place to start anyway.

"I'm sorry, Mari." The words spilled out as she bent near, tending a smaller slash on his upper chest, just below the collar bone. Her startled gaze flew upward to meet his. He had her attention, he only wished he knew what to say to make things right. "I'm sorry for not saying goodbye. I should have made a clean break rather than leave you hanging."

"Why did you?" The echoes of remembered pain in her unguarded expression sent a wave of sorrow through his heart. He had hurt her worse than he'd thought.

Simon sighed. "It wasn't anything you did, sweetheart. I just…I thought it was best to end things. I guess I hoped you would move on when I didn't come back."

Silence met his statement and he saw anger begin to simmer in her expression. "I waited for you, Simon. When you said you had to go, I thought you'd be back after your mission ended. Remember how I didn't ask any questions about where you were going or when you'd be back? I knew better than to ask, but then when you didn't return, I thought maybe you'd taken my silence as lack of interest."

Oh, he'd known she was interested. It had nearly killed him to leave her, but he hadn't seen any other choice at the time. Not after he'd recovered from that last mission. Everything had changed too much by then. He could never go back. Not then and not now.

"I'm sorry." It was too little, too late. The apology was all he had to offer and he knew it wasn't enough.

She turned away. "Yeah, me, too. Sorry I ever met you." Her words were pitched low, but he heard them…and felt them, like a knife to his gut.

He didn't know what he would have said in reply because at that moment the curtain of his cubicle was swept summarily aside and a Navy commander swept in. Not just any Navy commander, this man was an old friend and the commander he had been tasked to work under on his current mission.

"Where are your weapons, Si?" Commander Matthew Sykes didn't pull his punches. He was a man on a mission and all business while danger was a possibility. And they both knew Simon's weapons were more than run of the mill, and highly classified. That was precisely why he hadn't brought them inside the clinic.

"Stashed in the bushes outside the good doctor's office window." Simon nodded toward Mariana, one raised eyebrow making Matt aware of her presence and the need to be circumspect in front of her.

Matt snapped a look at his aide who had followed close behind, and the young seaman scurried off to secure the top secret darts. The creatures Simon was hunting could only be destroyed by a special, super strong toxin, and it was kept under lock and key except when Simon was in the field.

"Sorry for the intrusion, Doctor," Matt spoke to Mariana for the first time, and Simon didn't like the interest in his old buddy's expression.

"No problem, sir."

"How is he?" Matt asked Mariana about his status rather than talk to Simon directly, which annoyed him to no end. He had spent too many weeks being talked over by medical personnel to have any patience with it now.

"He lost a lot of blood and required a few stitches. His prognosis is good. I believe he'll be good as new in a few days. I'd like him to go to the base hospital for observation. He may still need a transfusion, though he's responding well."

"No hospital," Simon said quickly. Matt, thankfully, agreed with him.

"Only if it's absolutely necessary, Doctor. I'd prefer to keep this quiet. In fact, I'd prefer you didn't discuss his treatment with anyone else, and make no record of his visit to your clinic, if possible. His position here on base is—"

"Classified." Mariana dared to cut off the superior officer, a bored expression on her face. "I understand, sir. Simon and I know each other from his Spec Op days. He told me he's a civilian now and I can extrapolate from that."

Matt's eyes narrowed. "Then you understand his presence here is on a need-to-know basis."

"And I don't need to know. Got it, sir. I'll keep him here and observe him myself, then send him on his way if there are no complications."

Again Matt watched her, an uncertain expression on his face. They had been friends too long for Simon not to realize Matt was intrigued by her.

"I'd like a verbal report on his condition this evening, Doctor. Call my office and speak to no one except me. Understood?"

"Yes, sir."

"And Simon, I want you to stay here as long as necessary. I'll have Johnson bring over your kit before dark, just in case. In the meantime, get some rest."

"Sure thing, Matt." They'd been friends too long for Simon to be awed by Matt's rank. If Simon had stayed in the service, no doubt they would be equals at this point, having come up together through the ranks.

The commander left without further ado and Simon was left with Mariana once more.

"Want to tell me what that was all about?" A raised eyebrow dared him.

"Honey, you know I can't." The easy smile on her face said she was just teasing him and the idea that she would deal so easily when confronted by the very real secrecy he had to live with was surprising. He wouldn't have thought she'd take it so well.

"Fair enough. How are you feeling? Still light-headed?"

"I never said I was light-headed."

"You didn't have to say it, Simon. You were pale as a sheet when you wobbled onto that table. If you can walk, I have a more comfortable berth for you in back. You can catch some sleep and I'll check on you during the day to be sure you're bouncing back the way I expect. Sound good?"

"I've slept on some pretty hard ground over the years. Still, I wouldn't turn down a soft mattress if one is available." He levered himself upward with her assistance. He was still a touch dizzy, but he wouldn't let that stop him. She held his arm and his other hand went to the rolling IV pole as she guided him down the short corridor to a back room.

"We use this cot when we need to work late or do double shifts when there are large numbers of men in the field. It doesn't happen often, but it's there if we need it and right now, I think you need it most. Nobody will disturb you back here. The head is just down the hall. You should probably wait for one of us to assist you before you decide to walk any distances. Just in case."

"You'll have to tell your nurses not to discuss my presence. My mission is top secret, Mari."

He stopped just inside the door to gaze down at her. She was a head shorter than him but somehow they'd always managed to fit together like matching jigsaw pieces. When they'd made love, the experience had been transformational. Transcendent, even. Like nothing he had ever experienced before, and probably would never experience again.

"I'll take care of it. Don't worry. Margaret and Nancy are trustworthy. These days, medical professionals are held to a very high standard of patient privacy. Your treatment falls under that category."

He nodded, unable to look away from her beautiful face. The moment stretched. He had one hand on the IV pole and his uninjured arm resting on her shoulder. It took very little effort to pull her unresisting body closer, until they were only a breath apart.

God, how he'd missed the feel of her, the touch and scent of her. He needed…just one taste. That's all. One taste to hold against the future without her. Simon dipped his head, her lips so close to his own.

And then, he kissed her. He did the thing he had promised himself he would never do again. He kissed her, getting lost in the magic of her, her soft sighs, her delicate flavor, her luscious curves that fit so tightly against him.

For a split second, time stopped. She was in his arms and all was right with his world—for just a moment out of time. Then reality came crashing back as voices came down the hall. More staff arriving for their shift made a racket as they sought their desks, just beyond the wall that separated this back room from the rest of the small infirmary.

Mariana drew back, out of his arms, and he had to let her go. He hated to do it, but he knew damned well he had overstepped. The condemnation he feared he would see on her face would undo him. Instead of anger, he read the same startled deer-in-the-headlight response he was feeling. She would get mad later, he supposed, but for now, she was just as affected by their kiss as he was.

They'd never lacked chemistry. They'd had that going for them, at least. Still, there was too much else wrong with the relationship—with him—for there to be any possibility of a future together. Simon knew he would die a single man. No way would he subject any woman to the uncertainty that loomed in his future.

Mariana backed away from Simon, shocked nearly senseless by his kiss. It had always been that way with him. Explosive, almost mindless passion that sent her to the moon and back with nearly instantaneous motion. God, that man could kiss. And make love. She had dreamed about his lovemaking in the months since they'd parted.

He'd hurt her by leaving without a word and she didn't know if she could ever forgive him. By his actions and words, she didn't even know if he wanted to be forgiven. She didn't know what that kiss had been all about. Had it been just an impulse? Or had it been some deeper overture?

Did he want to get back together? Or did he merely want to tease her again, work her up into a frenzy of need, want, and desire, only to leave her without a backward glance again?

The bastard.

He had disappeared once. He would do it again in a heartbeat. She knew that like she knew the back of her hand. He had been a Spec Ops soldier, and was now a civilian contractor, which was a polite term for a soldier of fortune. A good, old-fashioned mercenary. Likely he was even worse now about commitment than he had been when he'd still been officially employed by Uncle Sam.

She needed to be wary. And she needed to stay away from him. No more kisses. No more tantalizing glimpses into what could have been...if only he'd returned to her.

This wasn't a return. It was a matter of coincidence that he needed medical help and she was the nearest doctor. If not for his injury, she suspected he never would have revealed his presence. He had probably done all he could to avoid running into her.

"How long have you been here at Quantico, Simon?"

He stepped back farther, in clear retreat. "About four months."

She should have known. Mariana just looked at him for a long moment, shaking her head as she mentally called herself all kinds of fool.

"Well." She had to get out of this room and he needed to lay down before he fell down. She took charge of his rolling IV stand and ushered him toward the bed. It wasn't grand. More of a cot, really. But it would do. She helped him arrange the arm with the IV in it, and waited until he found a comfortable position, tucking a sheet over his legs and up to his waist. He could tug it higher if he was cold. The infirmary was usually a little warmer than most of the other offices on base. "I'll check on you every half hour until I'm sure you're out of the woods. Try to sleep. If you need anything, just call. My office is next door. I'll hear you."

He grabbed her hand before she could bolt for the door.

"I won't apologize for kissing you, Mari. I will admit I was wrong to do it, though. I won't touch you again. Okay?"

He seemed to be seeking absolution. It was the least she could do for him so he would rest easy. And if he kept his word and didn't throw her into a tizzy again, it'd be worth it. He was too dangerous to her peace of mind.

"Okay. Get some rest, Si. I'll be back in a bit to see how you're doing."

CHAPTER 2

Simon's eyes snapped open the moment she walked into the room about twenty-five minutes later. He had always been a light sleeper, Mari remembered. She'd heard that Spec Ops guys trained for that sort of thing.

"Feeling any better?" She kept her voice deliberately low, in deference to his awakening senses. She also didn't want any of the other clinic workers to realize he was back here, per the commander's orders.

"Much better, thanks. You don't need to check on me. All I need now is sleep and I'll be fine."

She gave him a teasing smile as she advanced into the room. "Oh. I guess I thought I was the doctor here. Just let me take a quick set of vitals, check my needlework, and then I'll leave you to sleep."

She reached for the edge of his bandages, but he caught her wrist in a firm grip, shocking her gaze upward to meet his.

"I'm fine, Mari. Seriously."

"Well, *seriously*, Si. I need to check your condition. By rights, I should've sent you to the hospital for observation at the very least." He stared her down, apparently unwilling to let go of her hand. She recognized a brick wall when she met one. Mariana sighed and relaxed her stance. "Come on, Simon. You know you can trust me. What's up with you? Why won't you let me take care of you?"

"You already did, Mari." His whispered words reach right into her heart. "And I do trust you. It's why I came here last night instead of heading for the base hospital. I knew you'd patch me up and not ask too many questions."

"Oh, so that's your angle." She gave him a cunning smile as she perched on the side of his cot. "Buttering me up won't make me drop the subject. I *will* check your stitches and I *will* read your vitals. I'm the doctor here, Simon, lest you forget. *You* came to *me* for help. I'm not going to leave my job half done." He still hadn't let go of her wrist, making for close quarters as she sat next to him. "And it should go without saying that doctor-patient privilege holds. I won't discuss anything private about your condition or treatment with anyone. The only one I'm authorized to discuss your fitness with is your CO and I've already promised to call him later with an update. If you trust me enough to treat you, you should trust my discretion as well."

Simon seemed to think about it for a long moment, then finally let go of her wrist and lay back, flat on the small bed. The cot was barely large enough to hold his muscular frame, but she recognized the signs of intense fatigue. A person could sleep just about anywhere when they were as tired as he was. She had seen it before in troops undergoing combat training.

Simon's circumstances puzzled her. He seemed to be working alone and was no longer an official member of the military. A lone former Special Forces soldier, working clandestinely on one of the nation's most high-profile military bases, showing all the signs of having been living in the field and working hard on whatever mission he'd been given. It didn't make a lot of sense.

Even more troubling was Commander Sykes's unusual interest and the prohibitions he had given her against speaking about Simon's presence or condition. Something was definitely up, but it looked like she was the only one, aside from the commander and Simon, who had any idea that something was going on. What it was, she had no clue.

When Simon didn't make any further objections, she reached over and flicked on the bedside light so she could see him better. A few of the minor cuts had been left uncovered and they looked remarkably good. In fact, as she took a closer look, most of them seemed completely healed.

Impossible.

She adjusted the light closer and looked again. The minor scratches were gone.

Mariana felt chills run down her spine as she reached for the bandages that covered the worst of his wounds. She felt Simon's attention focus on her as she lifted the edge of the largest gauze pad. The stitches were still there, but the gaping gash beneath was now only a thin red line.

Mariana sat back, pulling the bandages completely off.

"What's going on here, Simon?"

"Mari, I…" He grimaced as if not sure what to say. He took his time deciding how to explain what she was looking at. "I was changed."

Her gaze shot to his, searching for meaning in his vague words. "Changed how? Did you volunteer for some kind of experiment? I've heard rumors about accelerated healing projects, but I've never seen anything like this."

"I didn't volunteer. I was affected by an injury on a mission. I nearly died. It was a close thing for a while, from what they told me later. I pulled through and this is one of the side effects. I heal really fast now."

"When?" Facts were spinning and colliding in her mind. "When did this happen to you?"

"On the mission right after I left you. I was sick for a long time and when I was finally well again, I…I thought you'd be better off without dealing with something like this. There's still a lot of uncertainty surrounding my condition."

"Oh, God, Simon." She was devastated by his words. He had left her without a backward glance—or so she'd thought.

Now perhaps, she understood why he'd never said goodbye.

"You can't talk about this, Mari."

There he went with the secrecy thing again. Sometimes she really hated the fact that he was a covert operator. The compartmentalization in his life was maddening.

She had to think. She had to regroup. She had to check his vitals and reassure herself that he truly was in as good condition as he seemed. She wouldn't let him leave later today if there was any danger of internal bleeding or complications from the blood loss he's sustained earlier. He looked really good on the surface, but she needed hard facts and numbers to be sure he was as healthy on the inside as he looked on the outside.

"All right." She rested her palms on her thighs and took stock, breathing deeply to regain some measure of sanity. "Let me take your vitals and then I'll get out of your way so you can get more sleep. You were beat when you showed up on my doorstep and I'll be damned if I let you go until you've caught up at least a little on your beauty rest."

He smiled at that. Just a small smile. It touched her deeply nonetheless. Simon's rare smiles had always had that effect on her, which was why she had tried so hard to earn them.

She reached for the blood pressure cuff and thermometer she had brought in with her and proceeded to take his readings. She occupied herself for the next few minutes with routine chores that told her what she needed to know about his inner condition.

"I hardly believe it. Your numbers are good, Si. Almost too good." She watched him with near disbelief as he bunched a pillow behind him and sat up to face her.

"I told you it would be okay. Please don't freak out on me, Mari."

"If I haven't freaked out yet, I'm not going to, but I won't lie to you. This is just plain weird. Have you had any other complications from that injury?"

He closed up. "I can't talk about it. I shouldn't have told you this much."

Damn, she kept running up against that wall of secrecy. Ultimately, she realized only now, the clandestine nature of his work and experiences had been a major challenge in their relationship. She cursed it. Yet in the same moment she knew that without his commitment to duty he wouldn't have been the same man she had grown to love. He was an elite soldier who lived by a sacred code of honor that she respected as much as she respected him.

And she still admired his commitment, honor, loyalty, and service, even though it had come between them. Knowing what she knew now—along with everything she suspected about his condition that he couldn't come out and tell her—her heart thawed. He had left her to spare her. Or what he perceived as being for her own good. He had always put her welfare first. It was maddening at times, as well as being incredibly sweet.

"So I guess my next question is, do you want me to take out the stitches now so you can sleep easier, or wait and do it tonight? Fair warning, it'll be easier now, while the wounds are still healing. I'm afraid if we wait it might hurt more."

"Then now it is." Simon gave her another tiny lift of one corner of his mouth. The man didn't fear pain, but he also wasn't stupid. The mixture of cunning and bravery had drawn her to him from the beginning and it was no less potent now.

"I'll just get a few things and be right back. Do you want me to bring back anything? Maybe some juice or water?"

"Juice would be good."

Or, maybe a seven-course meal with her luscious body for dessert. Simon kept that thought carefully to himself. Being around Mariana again was playing havoc with his control. He'd thought he could handle it, but he'd been wrong. Mari was his Achilles' heel. She got to him like no other woman ever had, or likely ever would.

He'd just shared one of his deepest secrets with her and she had barely blinked an eye. In all the scenarios he'd run in his mind, he never would've expected her relatively calm acceptance of the freak he'd become. She was made of even stronger stuff than he had thought.

She returned a few minutes later. She had a big bottle of orange juice in one hand and a small pan full of instruments, gauze, and what looked like small bottles of liquid in the other. He guessed the medicine bottles probably contained a topical anesthetic of some kind and maybe a disinfectant. Mari was a thorough and careful physician with a truly healing touch. He had always admired her skill and way with people.

She handed him the juice wordlessly, then adjusted the bedside light before sitting once more on the edge of his temporary berth. There wasn't much room on the small cot, so her thigh and hip pressed against his side.

He longed to stroke her skin with no barriers of cloth between them, but knew it was impossible. He'd made his choice when he'd left her. There would be no second chances for them. Not after what had happened to him.

Still the heat of her body pressing against his, even in this innocent way, brought back memories and longings best forgotten. How she had moved under him. How she had cried out when he made her come. How beautiful she always was when they made love and after, with her dark hair spread out over his pillow.

She was the most feminine, graceful woman he had ever known. Yet he knew her as a capable officer, brilliant doctor, and cunning opponent whenever they battled wits. Her tastes in music and films ran parallel to his, though she did tend to like the odd chick flick. Still, she didn't object to his penchant for horror movies too strenuously, so they'd rubbed along well together.

Then his life had actually *become* a horror movie and he knew he couldn't subject her to any of it. He would die before he saw her in danger. Especially danger he brought to her doorstep because of his work. No, she was better off without him in her life. Nothing would convince him otherwise, no matter how badly he wanted to take her in his arms and wish the world away.

He opened the juice bottle, busying his hands while she worked. She bathed the area in a liquid that tingled and then began snipping and tugging at the neat stitches she had put in him just an hour before. By tonight, if precedent held, he would be good as new, with not a scar in sight. Freak that he now was.

"This may hurt a little. Let me know if you want some more anesthetic."

"Just do it, baby. I've had worse."

Damn, his voice sounded rough. He needed to get a grip here. Her nearness was wreaking havoc with his libido…and his control. He hadn't bedded a woman since her. None since the attack that had made him what he was now.

A zombie hunter. A damned zombie magnet. The only thing that stood between the real world and the world of nightmares.

"I'd rather not hurt you if I can help it." She sounded more than a little annoyed. "No matter how much of a tough guy you are. You have nothing to prove here, Simon."

Oh yeah, she was annoyed. He'd always thought she was cute when she got uptight about something, which only annoyed her more, of course. Simon wisely kept silent but damn if she wasn't still the most complex, engaging, and attractive woman he had ever known. Even when she was pissed off at him.

"How does that feel?" She'd finished with one row of stitches and was on to the next.

"Fine, doc. Just keep going. I'll let you know if there's a problem."

She shot him a disgusted look. Still, he could see the worry that tightened the tiny lines around her eyes. It touched him that even after the way he had left her, without even saying goodbye, she still cared. At least a little. At least enough not to want to cause him unnecessary pain.

Of course, she was a doctor. It might have something to do with her Hippocratic oath. She would probably do the same for anyone. Even her worst enemy. Even the man who'd left her without a word of farewell.

Simon tried to live his life without regrets but the way he had dealt with Mariana was one of his biggest. He felt guilty about what he'd done—or rather what he *hadn't* done. Not saying goodbye was a cowardly move and he wasn't proud of his past actions.

Maybe this was his chance to finally make it right. When he'd first been hired to do this job, he had scoped out what he would do if he was hurt. The base hospital was out of the question. Once a military doctor saw what his body could do now, Simon would never be free of them. He wouldn't go down that road if he could help it.

When he'd learned of Mariana's field clinic he knew that was his only option. One he wouldn't take unless there was no other alternative. Last night, his choice had been taken away and now he had to make the best of it.

That he could trust her went without question. He knew her to be a woman of deep integrity. Even after what he'd done, she wouldn't betray him. He was glad he finally had a chance to apologize for his cowardly actions and maybe help her heal from the injury he'd dealt.

As she finished with the last of the stitches, he captured her hand. "How have you been, Mari?"

She seemed surprised by his question, but less annoyed than she had been a moment ago. "Better than you, from what I've seen today."

He had to laugh at her wry humor. The tightness around her eyes eased some more.

"You've got me there." He let go of her hand. "I meant what I said before. I'm sorry for the way I left without a word. It was wrong."

"It was," she agreed readily as she collected her things back into that curved pan. "I think I understand why you did it a little better now. I just wish…"

"What?" He wasn't sure he really wanted to know, but had to ask.

"I wish you'd trusted me. I don't know. Maybe I could

have helped. I'm a pretty good researcher. Maybe I could have found something to help you."

Her words surprised him, though on reflection, they shouldn't have. She had been part of a military research study when they'd met. She had a brilliant mind and a stellar reputation as a medical professional. She probably would have done all she could to help him, had he told her the true nature of his condition.

The military didn't even know everything about the changes to his body, and he was careful to keep it that way. As far as they knew, he'd gained immunity to the contagion only. They didn't know about the other side effect of his run-in with the monsters they had created. He'd been lucky up to this point. He hadn't learned of the super fast healing until after he was out of the service and being treated by a civilian doctor.

"I'm okay, Mari. Really. I have a doctor I trust and he says I'm stable for the moment."

"For the moment?" She sounded suspicious and a little annoyed. He could tell she didn't like that last part at all.

"It's the best he could do given what happened to me. We're breaking new ground here, Mari. For what it's worth, I prefer to do it on my own, without being a lab rat."

"Si, you know I would never—" She looked so affronted it was actually cute. He cut her off by placing one finger over her luscious lips.

"I trust you with my life, Mari. That's why I came here when I got hurt and didn't trek over to the base hospital. I figured if I could trust anyone on this base, it was you, even after what I'd done. I'm gratified to know I was right, but I can't say I'm surprised." For once, he hoped his expression conveyed what he was feeling. "You've always had my utmost respect."

She tilted her head, considering him for a long moment. "And you will always have mine, Simon." Her low voice sent shivers down his spine all out of proportion with the conversation, but then all Mariana had to do was breathe to turn him on. She stood and gathered her supplies. "Get some rest. I'll check on you in a few hours and bring you some food. How does roast beef on rye sound?"

"Delicious. You remembered." He still remembered all her favorite things, too. Like her favorite positions for making love, her favorite places to be touched, and her favorite techniques for making him absolutely crazy with need. But those were better left alone for now. He didn't deserve her. He had never deserved her. All he had now were memories and he would have to be content with them.

"I remember a lot of things, Simon." The heat that flared in her dark eyes told him her agile mind might be tracking along the same path as his.

That was a danger zone, fraught with trouble for them both. He backed off, yawning to break the sudden sexual tension that lay thick in the air. He was drained both physically and emotionally after the physical rigors of the night before and the confrontation with Mari he had put off too long. He wasn't really faking the yawn. His body needed to recharge in a big way.

She let it slide, backing away and heading for the door. "Sleep well, Simon. I'll be back in a couple of hours."

Knowing he would see her again, Simon followed orders and sank into a dreamless sleep on the almost-comfortable cot.

CHAPTER 3

As it turned out, the clinic was a madhouse for the rest of the day. Mariana was able to sneak in back a few times to peek in and make sure Simon was okay, but that was all she had time for. When one of the nurses went out to get food, she asked her to bring back the roast beef on rye with all the works, plus a salad.

The sandwich was for Simon, the salad for herself. She took a half hour to go in back around two o'clock in the afternoon to find Simon dozing. He woke as soon as she entered and sat up. They ate together, talking about commonplace things and old times. It was light conversation. With the noise from the clinic in the distance, she was just as glad not to get into anything too heavy with him while they ate.

She looked at his wounds once more, shocked by the clear flesh that met her inspection. Not even a scratch marred his skin. Chills went down her spine as she realized how radically his body chemistry must have been altered by whatever had happened to him. He was right to stay clear of any doctor who might not have his best interests at heart.

Simon could all too easily become some selfish doctor's lab rat. If the changes in his body could be studied—if the healing power he possessed could be harnessed—well, it would make someone very rich indeed. It could also be something the military establishment could use to make their soldiers nearly invulnerable. It could be something truly huge. And something very dangerous for Simon, since he was the only one in the world to possess such abilities at the moment.

He was much better off keeping it a secret for now. For all she knew, it could be a temporary condition. It might dissipate on its own. Or it might morph yet again into something that could kill him.

She wished he had come to her in the beginning. She wished he would let her help him more than by just patching up his cuts. But it was his life. His decision. She wouldn't pressure him. She just wanted him to know she would be there if he ever needed her help.

"I'm going to call Commander Sykes and make my report. I'm going to tell him you're much improved and will be on your way back to his command after the clinic closes for the day."

"That sounds about right. After this most excellent lunch, I'll probably sleep a few more hours. If Matt Sykes sends over one of his guys with my stuff, I can duck out of here right after your staff leaves for the night."

She wished he'd stay, but knew her reasons were purely selfish. "I'll let him know."

"Mari," his tone grew serious as he drew her attention. "Matt doesn't know about the healing. If you could avoid telling him everything…"

"Never fear. I, of all people, can see the potential problems for you if news of your condition got out. I'll tell the commander that you're good to go and that's all he needs to know."

"You're a peach, Mari." The grin her sent her reminded her of their dating days. It was too close to flirting for her comfort.

Mariana stood, gathering up the trash. "I'll let you rest. If you need anything, you know where to find me."

"Thanks, Mari. For everything." The moment stretched and felt just a little too serious. Then he grinned again. "And especially for remembering my favorite sandwich. I've been living off field rations for a few weeks. That roast beef tasted like a little slice of heaven."

He rubbed his stomach with a silly expression on his face and she knew he'd done it to make her laugh. She couldn't help herself. Simon was his most charming when he didn't take himself too seriously. It hadn't happened often, but once in a while he'd unbent enough to act the clown. Just for her.

She left him, still chuckling, and headed for her office to make the promised call to Commander Sykes. She was careful to give the commander the bare facts, not delving into the details of Simon's physical condition, only assuring Sykes that he was fit for duty and would be leaving the clinic that night after closing time. Sykes seemed satisfied with that and Mariana breathed a sigh of relief.

Sykes reminded her there were to be no records of Simon's treatment or even his presence on base. For once, Mariana was grateful for the clandestine nature of Simon's work. No one would hear of his healing abilities from her—or even know he'd been in her clinic. She trusted her nurses not to say anything, so Simon was in the clear for this incident. She only hoped he would be as lucky the next time he got hurt.

He slept the afternoon away while Mariana finished up her day in the clinic. It had been a busier day than usual and Simon's presence upset her emotional equilibrium. She locked the clinic door behind the last nurse to leave and went back to see how he was doing. A young officer had come over a half hour earlier to drop off a big black duffel full of stuff for Simon's eyes only. She'd directed the man to the back and he had come and gone without much more ado.

Mariana tapped on the doorframe, hearing movement from within. "Simon?"

"Come on in, Mari." She heard rustling as she entered and realized he was stuffing his old clothing into the duffel. He had changed into fresh camo BDUs and managed a quick shave. Damn, the man looked good enough to eat.

She'd been down that road before. No matter how much she missed him, and though she knew now why he had left without a word, she wasn't sure she was ready to risk her heart again. He'd broken it once already.

"I just locked up. Everyone's gone for the night."

"Then I'll be going, too. There's not much time before sunset."

She wondered why that mattered. Then again, he'd been on night duty when he'd gotten hurt. Whatever he was doing out there in the woods, it was a nighttime thing. Maybe he had a squad he had to get back to, waiting for him in the trees. She wouldn't ask, no matter how curious she was.

"I can drop you off wherever you want." She thought she would at least make the offer, though he wasn't likely to take her up on it.

"Are you heading right home? No errands to run or places to go tonight?"

She was puzzled by his question, though she saw no harm in answering him truthfully. "No place to go tonight. I'm heading home to do laundry actually."

He lifted the bulging duffel bag as she watched him from near the door. "That's good. Mari…" he stepped close to her, his expression intent, "…until my mission is complete, stay close to home at night. It's safer."

"Is there something I should worry about?"

"Just trust me. I can't say more. Just stay inside while the sun's down."

Frankly, she was surprised he'd gone that far. Whatever he was doing in the woods at night, it was dangerous. Dangerous enough for him to warn her when he was probably sworn to secrecy. Now *that* gave her pause.

"All right, Simon. I'll be more cautious after dark."

He prowled over to her in that silent way of his. He moved into her personal space before she could say another word and one of his big hands touched her cheek. He towered over her and something in his eyes made her feel…odd. Not quite the way she used to feel in his presence—totally overwhelmed and as if he was her past, present and future—but protected…cherished…and regretted.

It was bittersweet.

He didn't say a word as his head dipped and his mouth claimed hers in a poignant farewell. Tears started behind her eyes. She wasn't sure if she would ever see him again after this and the kiss he gave her had a sense of heartbreaking finality to it.

Her hands went to the lapels of his shirt as she pressed herself against his muscular chest. He hadn't changed much since she'd last seen him. Not in any outward way. It was the internal changes that gave her pause.

Simon drew back, holding her gaze. There was something indefinable in his gaze that touched her deeply. The silence stretched as he looked at her and she wondered what thoughts passed through that agile brain of his.

"Stay safe, Mari."

The moment ended and she stepped back. "I'll be fine, Simon. Watch yourself when you're out there. If you need anything, you know where to find me."

"I need a lot of things, Mari." His expression smoldered. "Most of which I can't have."

"Can't you?"

"No." The word hung between them for a timeless moment, then he moved, breaking the spell.

Simon opened the door and held it open for Mariana to precede him. They walked the short distance to the clinic entrance before they both paused once more while she unlocked the door.

"Will I see you again?" Damn, she hadn't meant to ask. She cringed inwardly at how needy she sounded.

"It's not a good idea." His eyes clouded with an emotion she couldn't interpret as the moment dragged.

"I understand." It seemed the right thing to say.

"No you don't." His smile was almost her undoing. "And I can't tell you any more than I already have. You'll just have to trust me."

"I do. I've always trusted your judgment as far as my safety goes, Simon. I think you're wrong about other things. In particular, I think you're wrong about us."

Their eyes locked. "You don't know how much I wish I were."

He gave her one last, hard kiss, then left her standing in the empty doorway. She watched him walk off, into the setting sun. It was sort of poetic, in a way.

In all other ways, it just plain sucked.

Simon was gone within moments, disappearing into the tree line. She doubted she would ever see him again. Her breath caught in her throat as that realization struck home.

It had been an upsetting day all the way around. She'd discovered things about him—about what had happened to him—that made her want to cry. For him. For the things he'd been through. The uncertainty about his condition, the threat to his life. She hated that he'd had to go through that alone and longed to be let into his life so she could help in whatever way possible.

Simon was a tough guy though. He had rarely opened up to her during their brief affair and now wasn't any different.

At the very least, she'd achieved some closure. Seeing him again and gaining insight into why he had disappeared before helped a little. It would take time to put everything in perspective but at least she wasn't left wondering.

Not about his abandonment anyway. No, now she would wonder about his health, his safety, whether or not he was alive or dead. She would wonder and worry for him. The man she had never gotten over. The lover she missed every single day.

She sighed heavily and left the clinic, heading for her car. The sun was sinking behind the trees and she'd promised him she would stay in tonight. She didn't understand why it was so important to him, but she had felt the urgency in his words, in his stare. So, she would go home and do this last thing for him. It was little enough. This one last thing and then she would do her best to put Simon Blackwell behind her. Forever.

*

Walking away from Mariana again was one of the hardest things he had ever done. Of course, he didn't see any other way to keep her truly safe. He faded into the trees, then doubled back, watching as she made her way out of the clinic and into her car. When she pulled out and headed for home, he went back into the deeper woods and began a jogging pace. He decided to go toward the area near her housing unit.

He would check that she made it home safely, then begin his nightly patrol. The search area had grown closer and closer to her backyard lately as the creatures started to go farther and farther afield. That wasn't good. He'd vowed to contain them. Failure was not an option. Especially not with Mariana's safety in question.

A little more than an hour later, Simon peered through the trees at Mariana's home, watching her move around behind the windows. She was home. Safe for now.

It was time to go hunting.

*

Mariana tried her best to put the disturbing thoughts of her encounter with Simon out of her head as she ate dinner, but found it impossible. He was never far from her mind. She had learned so much today. Still, she knew so little. His healing was nothing short of miraculous. He had hinted at something horrific that had brought it about and she wanted to know more. She also knew he would never tell. Not unless there was no other choice.

She would either have to be read into the program—

which was as likely as a snowball in hell right about now—or she would have to discover what had happened to him on her own somehow. Another fat chance. In all likelihood, she would never know what had brought about his amazing change. She might not ever see him again either. It was that last thought that brought a tear to her eye.

She had loved him so deeply. He had taken up residence in her soul and she realized only now, after seeing him again, that he'd never quite left. She still loved him and cared about what happened to him. Even if they could never be together, she wanted to be sure he was safe. And she wanted him to be happy.

He hadn't looked all that happy today. Dark shadows filled his eyes—even darker than they had been before. His face had been leaner, harder than she remembered, though his physique hadn't suffered. He was still built like a Greek god with a casual attitude about his amazing shape. He used his body as a tool in his work. He hadn't perfected that physique by standing in front of a mirror in a gym somewhere. To her, that was a plus. Simon was unconsciously sexy. A warrior first, whose body was a honed weapon.

Just remembering what he could do with that killer bod made her quiver. They had been together far too short a time, in her opinion. She could have spent years making love to him and still not be satisfied. He had ruined her for anyone else.

With a sigh, Mariana finished her lonely dinner and began cleaning up. She spent some time by the sink, washing the dishes that had stacked up over the past few days. She lived alone, so she could afford to be a little lax on the household chores if her work schedule interfered.

Her cabin was rustic, but she loved it. She had taken her time choosing it, wanting something closer to nature than she had ever had before. Hers was the only house on the lane, with her nearest neighbors out of sight over a small hill. The neighbors were quiet, an elderly lady and her granddaughter who took care of her. Mariana had visited them a few times since moving in, but mostly they kept to themselves.

Mariana's backyard was small compared to other places she had lived. It bordered the woods so it felt like the whole forest was her backyard at times. Deer often came out of the woods to nibble on her lawn and there were all kinds of birds and little furry creatures that visited from time to time.

There was a small window over the sink and as dusk turned to deep night, she watched the woods as she worked, noting the appearance of a few small woodland creatures. An owl hooted and she thought she caught the flash of its eyes in one tall pine, but couldn't be certain.

Turning back to her task, she concentrated on the dishes for a while. When she looked up again, the woods were dark, mysterious, and silent. Not a single creature stirred. A predator of some kind must be nearby. The smaller animals always knew when something bigger and badder was around.

She shut off the water and wiped her hands, raising her gaze to take one last look out the window.

She froze, a scream stuck in her throat as a face—a gruesome face—reflected back at her from the other side of the window.

Was it a trick of the light? Was she looking at her own reflection, somehow distorted into a grotesque mask? Or was there someone—or some*thing*—out there, looking back at her?

She dropped to a crouch, using the kitchen counter for cover as her breathing spiked in panic. What to do? Her cell phone was plugged in to the charger in the other room. Her rifle was in the hall closet, unloaded. She had a few kitchen carving knives in the drawer behind her, but she wasn't much of a hand-to-hand fighter. She'd had the training early in her career with the Navy, of course, but had only done enough to pass, never excelled.

She cursed her own inability and laziness. She had meant to better her skills. She'd just never gotten around to it. Something always had seemed to get in the way or be more important. Now she saw the folly in her delay. She would go tomorrow and sign up for a self-defense course. It was stupid to live way out here on her own with no real way to defend herself should someone try something.

If someone was really out there, she was a sitting duck. The more she thought about what she had seen in that flash of time, the more convinced she was that something really was out there. A person or maybe a few kids playing a trick of some kind, trying to scare the shit out of her. Well, they'd succeeded, if that was their aim. If not, what was up with the guy she'd seen?

And what was with that face? The quick glimpse she'd gotten looked like something had gnawed off parts of that horribly misshapen face. She was so frightened, yet felt silly. She didn't know if she had really seen what she thought she'd seen. Second guessing her senses, she still wasn't quite brave enough to stand up and take another look outside.

Instead, she listened carefully, every sense extended as she cowered behind the sink. Was that a creak? Did something just brush against the exterior of the house?

Oh, God.

This was ridiculous. Cowering there by the sink like a ninny was getting her no place. It was time to man up and go see what was really going on. For all she knew, it could really just be some local kids prowling around, hoping to scare the bejeezus out of someone. She'd be damned if she would be the one they snickered over in the woods.

Crawling forward, she plotted a path out of the kitchen that wouldn't expose her to view from the window. It involved climbing under the kitchen table, but she was okay with that. She could stand to lose a little dignity in exchange for safety—just in case it wasn't kids and there really was some sort of trespassing Peeping Tom outside her window.

Mariana headed for the hall closet first. Better to be armed and the phone was farther away. She felt marginally better with the rifle cradled in her arms, fully loaded and ready for action. Next, she grabbed her phone, dialing the emergency number as she moved toward the back door that faced the woods. She approached it at an oblique angle, trying to peer out the small window set into the door.

The phone seemed to work at first, then petered out and died. Not enough juice. Damn. She'd have to go back into the other room to get the charging cord and she didn't want to take the time. The more time that passed, the more she became convinced that she had to have been seeing things. No suspicious sounds came from outside and she couldn't see anything, or anyone, in her backyard. Maybe it had all been just a trick of the light. Or if it was kids, they were gone now that they'd succeeded in their prank.

Cautiously, she opened the back door and stepped onto the porch.

A second later she saw it, coming around the side of the house. It looked like a man in tattered camo fatigues, but its face…its face was…horrible.

Streaked with grime that didn't look like camo paint, bits of flesh hung off his jaw and gouges were taken out of his hollow cheeks. His eyes were vacant, staring. His jaw locked in position, seemingly unable to move.

Mariana stared. Her rifle lay in her arms, but she was unable to lift it—or even to think—as the thing came toward her.

"Get in the house!"

She knew that voice. Or rather, that shout. It was coming from the woods.

"Simon?" She peered into the darkness, looking for him. He broke through the cover of the trees a moment later. He ran toward her and the creature, weapons in hand.

"In the house, now!"

She didn't need further urging. Her body responded to the order in his tone, the urgency of his command. She fled, locking the door behind her and racing through the house, rifle in hand, to make sure all the other entrances were shut tight.

The windows were vulnerable, of course, but they were small enough that a full-grown man would have to shimmy through them carefully, if he even fit at all. It was a trade-off she'd made for safety, living alone out here in the woods. Smaller windows meant less light and a reduced view. When she had first seen the house and the tiny windows, she'd thought the decrease in light was worth the increase in protection, and that compromise was paying off now.

House as secure as she could make it, Mariana returned to the kitchen. She peeked out the window. No sign of the monster that had taken the form of a man. She gasped as a camo green covered chest filled her vision.

Simon was on her porch, in front of her door. Thank God.

"Is it clear?" she asked through the door.

"For the moment. Open up, Mari."

She did, flinging her arms around him as he stepped over the threshold. She heard him kick the door shut behind him and the dead bolt snick into place. Thankfully, he didn't let her go, even as he saw to their safety. She was shaking from head to toe and he was a solid, comforting presence.

Rifle barrel gripped tight in one hand, she clung to him, reaction setting in. After a moment she felt his arms settle around her shoulders, stroking her back as she shook.

"It's all right now, sweetheart. I took care of the problem. He won't trouble you again." His deep voice crooned to her, calming her further. At length, she stepped back.

Damn, he looked good. Whole and healthy once more. She never would have believed he'd be in such good shape after the way she had seen him, broken and bleeding only hours ago. His color was good, though his face was darkened in places with camo paint. He was all hunter, lean and alert, clearly on a mission.

"What was that? What did you do with him?"

"He's gone. That's all you need to know."

"More secrecy, Simon?" She hated the way her voice broke, her blood still running high with emotion. "I can't take much more, you know. Not now. Not after that guy scared the living shit out of me!"

"Whoa," he reached for her, tugging her into his arms again. "Calm down, honey. You're okay. He's gone and I'm here. I'll watch over you."

That sounded awfully possessive to her. And a little patronizing. But she was willing to let that slide for the moment as adrenaline rushed through her system.

"How did you know where I live?" His expression shuttered as she looked up at him, pulling out of his arms. "You've been watching my house, haven't you?"

She had her answer when he looked away. His face never betrayed his thoughts, but his eyes told stories. At least to her. She had always been able to uncover his feelings just by looking into his eyes.

"Damn it, Simon. Am I in danger out here?"

"Yes." Well, he certainly didn't pull his punches. She would give him that. "You should think hard about moving onto the base until this is all over. As you saw firsthand tonight, it isn't safe to be out here in the woods all by yourself."

"What the hell was that, Simon? I saw his face. He looked like…like some kind of monster. Like something had been eating his face!"

She'd seen more than he'd thought. More than he'd hoped. More than she should have.

"Come clean with me, Simon. You know I won't share classified information or blow your mission. I need to know what that was…and if there are more." The crack in her unsteady voice moved him.

He really shouldn't tell her. She had seen too much already. On the other hand, she was an experienced Naval officer with a distinguished record. He knew her personally, and knew she could be trusted. Furthermore, he knew her personality and that she was likely to try digging for answers on her own. That path could only lead to trouble.

For her sake, he would give her a little more information. It was a judgment call on his part, and he trusted her to be circumspect.

"There are more, Mari. That's why you need to get out of here. They come out at night. The sun makes them hide. Clouds and twilight are their friends. Whatever you do, don't go out in the woods when it's overcast, or at night. If they bite you, you're dead."

"What about if they bite *you?* God, Simon! Your mission is to take out these things, isn't it? That's why you're here and why everything is so hush-hush."

"You always were quick, Mari. And now you know way more than you should."

"But not nearly everything, I'll bet."

"I've said too much already."

"Who am I going to tell? You know I would never put you or your career in danger, Simon. I'll keep your secrets, but I'm worried for you and scared to death of what I just saw." She was still trembling. He hated seeing her in such a state. "You've been living in the woods, hunting these things, haven't you?"

He couldn't deny that. His bivouac was very close to her house, in fact. "I've been nearby," he hedged.

She crumpled, sinking into one of the kitchen chairs. "Then you might as well stay here during the day. This house is practically in the woods and built with security in mind. It's very hard for anyone to break in here once I lock up. Plus, after your injury—even with your new superpowers—you should be sleeping in a bed, not on the ground in the elements." He heard the sarcasm and the very real concern for his well-being in her voice.

He weighed his options. Her plan had merit, loath as he was to admit it. She worked during the day and wouldn't be in the cabin except on her days off. He worked nights on this mission and the cabin was convenient to his hunting grounds. The only thing that stopped him from accepting her offer was the possibility that he might bring more of the zombies to her door.

Of course, at least one of them seemed to have found her

on his own. That was a troubling development. But she was right about the house being secure. He'd scouted it himself when he first started working on this problem. The windows were too small for anyone to climb through and the doors—once bolted—wouldn't be easy to access. Her house was as safe as anywhere right now, as long as she didn't open a door.

Which was why he wasn't going to insist she move. Now that she knew about the problem, she'd be more careful. Mariana had always had a good head on her shoulders. The zombies though...their change in behavior was troubling. If they were ranging closer to the few houses that dotted this area, they were getting more adventurous. Not a good sign at all. He had to work fast before the infection spread any further.

"All right. I'll camp out on your porch during the day. At night, I'll expect you to either hole up tight inside or stay on base for your own safety. As you saw tonight, I can't be everywhere at once. This one slipped past me. I'm sorry, Mari." He hated to think what had almost happened. "If I'd been any later—"

"You weren't." She cut off his words with a gentle touch of one hand on his forearm. His compassionate lover was back, comforting him when she was the one truly in need of comfort. His Mari had a heart as big as the world. "Thank you for coming to my rescue."

"If one of them ever gets that close to you again, I want you to promise me you'll run, Mari. Regular bullets don't work on these guys. If they bite you, you'll die. Then you'll become one of them." Unspoken went the thought that he would have to destroy her if the worst happened. It would kill him.

"They're infectious?"

"Highly. The contagion is in their bite. And they really like to bite."

"You got bitten." Understanding dawned in her eyes. "That's what happened to you, isn't it?"

Grimly, he nodded. "I'm a one in a million case. I

survived. And I'm not a carrier. I'm not contagious and can't give it to anyone."

"That's why they sent you after these things."

"The contagion doesn't work on me. Something in my system gives me immunity, though it did make me very sick the first time. Since then, well, you saw the changes in my healing. That's what the stuff was designed to do, but…" He trailed off, realizing he was saying too much.

"But something went horribly wrong. Simon, this is terrible. Truly awful."

"You won't get an argument from me." He leaned back against the kitchen counter. "Look, I have to get back out there. I was tracking two more of them when I heard the commotion over here. They can't be far and I want to get them before they go to ground for the day."

"You've been doing this every night for the past four months?" He read the disbelief and horror on her beautiful face.

"I spent the first month scouting. These guys were once Marines. They still retain some of their knowledge and training, as far as I can tell. They know how to evade capture and hide in the woods."

"How many more are there?"

"Near as we can figure, just a few more. We've accounted for all but a handful of missing Marines. A few more weeks and I'll be done laying them to rest."

That made her pause. Those…things…had once been men. Marines, from what Simon had said.

"Did they volunteer for the initial experiment?" She was almost afraid of his answer—if he'd answer at all. He'd been surprisingly forthcoming so far, but she knew he hadn't told her everything. She also knew there were limits on how far he would go in briefing her.

"The group was made up of Marines who had fallen in battle with no family other than the Corps. They left their bodies to science and one of your colleagues in the medical world used them for the initial round of tests."

"They were reanimated after death?" The horror of that didn't bear thinking about, yet it had been done.

"An unintended consequence of what was supposed to have been a much simpler test. Something to do with cellular response. I'm no expert on the science part. I guess they figured there wasn't a need for any security on the lab. No need to protect a few dead bodies, right?" He paused and shivers coursed down her spine. "Then the corpses got up and walked out of the lab in the middle of the night. Being good soldiers, they headed for cover in the woods. Soon after, the first attacks began. A platoon of Marines was sent after them and only a few made it back. The rest became what you saw tonight. Me and my men were called in and we learned how to fight them. The science team came up with a toxin that disrupts the bioelectric connections that keep them going. They sort of disintegrate as their cells lose cohesion. It's the only thing that stops them. Regular bullets don't even slow them down. They feel no pain and can't really die. Because they're already dead." He straightened and checked his weapons. "I'm going to leave this with you." He handed her a pistol loaded with what looked like a dart. "Only use it if absolutely necessary. Aim for any exposed skin. The toxin works fast once delivered, but stay clear until the zombie disintegrates. That's the only way to be certain it's finished."

"Zombie? You're calling them that?" She was appalled.

He shrugged. "It seemed to fit. They're dead. They're walking around trying to eat people. Sounds just like one of those old horror movies to me."

"Good Lord." She took the weapon gingerly, checking the safety automatically. She noted his approving nod.

"Be very careful with the darts. The substance inside can kill you as easily as it does the zombies. It's highly classified and usually kept under lock and key unless I'm out hunting."

"That's why Commander Sykes was so keen to take control of your weapons while you were in the clinic."

"And why only his staff has access to the vault where my ammo is kept. I'm probably breaking a half dozen rules giving this to you." He impressed her with his serious mien. "I figure you're a doctor, you know how to handle toxic substances, and as we just saw, you're in the line of fire. If you won't agree to leave, you should at least have some protection."

"I'm not leaving."

"We'll argue more about that later." The slight roll of his eyes and lift of his lips told her he was taking her refusal better than she had expected. Simon could be very autocratic at times. Luckily, those times were rare.

"I'm not driving anywhere in the dark tonight with more of those things nearby. I think I'm safer here, for the time being at least."

"Fair enough. Just don't go opening the door again." He shook his head. "Look, I've got to go. Lock everything. Hunker down and lay low. I'll be back at dawn when they go to ground for the day. If you have any problems before then, call this number." He scribbled on a pad she kept on the counter near the door. "Put that in your speed dial. I have a cell phone set on vibrate. I'll feel it, even if I can't answer, and come running. Be vigilant." He paused by the door. "I don't like leaving you alone here."

"Go do your job, Si. I'll be all right until you get back. And I do know how to shoot. Remember?" Once upon a time, they'd shared a memorable afternoon at the shooting range followed by a spectacular night of lovemaking. It had been their third date and the first time they'd made love.

"I remember, Mari." In a lightning quick move he pulled her into his arms for a quick kiss that left her weak kneed. He let her go all too soon, while her world was still spinning. "Lock this after me and stay out of view of the windows. If they see you, they'll coming looking."

"Aye, aye, sir." She tried to hide how scared she really was. Scared, but she was staying in her house. She wouldn't abandon ship when Simon was out there, in danger. She would wait for him. Just like she had been waiting for him since he left the last time. Only this time, he'd promised to come back. She didn't know how long he would stay this time, but for at least one more day, he'd be in her world.

She was beginning to think any time with him was better than forever without him.

It was a dangerous path she was on, in more ways than one. He had broken her heart once already. More than likely, she was already setting herself up for another fall, and putting herself in harm's way just to be near him. If he didn't break her, the zombies just might.

CHAPTER 4

Simon returned just after dawn. Mariana hadn't been able to sleep a wink, but it didn't matter. She wasn't on duty today and didn't have to go anywhere.

She'd spent the night making a fortress out of her little cabin in the woods, barricading windows and covering them with curtains, blankets, and any kind of dark fabric she could find. She didn't want to be seen from outside as she moved around in the house. All the while, she had kept watch on the woods, dreading seeing another one of those monsters staring back at her. Or worse, seeing Simon emerge, covered in blood the way he had been the day before in the infirmary.

When he finally did show up, he looked tired. Tired and unharmed. Thank heaven. She let him in, surreptitiously looking him over to be sure he was truly all right.

"You're a sight for sore eyes," she admitted as he walked past her shouldering a small pack.

"Miss me?" He looked tense and a little grim even as he teased her.

"What's wrong?"

He paused, lowering his pack to the floor. "You always could read me like a book. Nobody else can, Mari. It's a little unnerving."

She was surprised by the moment of candor and decided to repay it in kind. "Nothing shows on your face, Simon. It's your eyes…I can read a whole story from the way they sparkle at me. It's subtle and it took me a while to figure out your secret code." She gave him a lopsided smile. "I doubt a casual acquaintance would be able to read you at all. Never fear." He regarded her for a minute more, then turned away. He was clearly uncomfortable with her words. It wasn't the first time she'd said something that made him wary and it likely wouldn't be the last. Not if he stuck around for any length of time. "Did you get your man?"

His lips tightened. "I got them both. It's…not easy to end them. They were Marines. They shouldn't have died this way."

She realized he was dealing with some serious emotional issues on this mission in addition to the danger and sheer weirdness factor. Mariana had thought about it all night while she had been cowering like a mouse in her cabin. She felt a certain amount of sympathy for the Marines who'd died only to become monsters, but the zombies themselves freaked her out. Big time.

"From the little I saw last night, it has to be done, Simon. They're lucky to have someone like you on the job." His compassion and insight didn't surprise her. She'd long suspected he had a sensitive soul hidden under that tough as nails exterior.

"Did you have any trouble here?"

He was changing the subject again. Her cue to let it go. For now, she would let him have his way.

"No trouble after you left. I took your advice and shored up the cabin even more. I made a place for you in the spare room."

"I'm happy on the porch. I don't need anything fancy."

"It's not fancy. It's just a bed, Simon. Why sleep outside on the porch when you can be more comfortable in a real bed just a few yards away?"

She motioned him toward the short hall off the kitchen

and he followed with his pack.

"So you're not leaving, I take it?"

"I've been thinking about it and I'm staying. From what you said, those things have been out in the woods for months now and I've never seen one until last night. Chances are, I'll be fine." She opened the door to the small guest room and preceded him into the tightly furnished space. The bed took up most of the area, with a little room to squeeze by to get to the chest of drawers and small table in one corner.

"I'd feel better if you stayed on base until this is over, Mari. The cabin itself is pretty safe, but you're still vulnerable going to and from." He had stopped in the doorway, crowding her into the small room with just his presence. She'd forgotten how huge he really was in comparison to her. He was overwhelming…in the most deliciously masculine way, of course.

"I'll consider it if there are further problems, but for right now, I'm staying put. I've barricaded and covered the windows. This place is sealed up tight and unless they have access to C4 or other high explosives, I doubt anyone will be able to get in here once I've shut it up tight for the night."

"The fact that you saw one of the zombies at all means they're getting more adventurous, ranging farther afield. It's not a good sign, Mari."

She couldn't respond to the appeal in his voice. She needed to be here, to be sure he came back every morning, to see him and talk to him. Maybe it was foolish, but she'd gone for months without seeing him and this might be her last chance to store up memories of Simon before he left again. If memories were all she could have of him, she wanted as many as possible to hold against the long, lonely future ahead.

"Don't ask me to leave, Si." Her voice whispered through the space between them, making the moment more intimate. Simon moved closer, holding her gaze.

"Mari, I didn't want you involved in this." She saw the caring in his expression, for once unguarded and open. "I worry for your safety. I'd die if anything happened to you."

He cupped her cheek as he moved closer still. Those were some pretty serious words and she knew he meant every syllable. They warmed her, as did the longing in his eyes.

"I could say the same for you, Simon. I worry about you. I don't ever want to see you covered in blood the way you were the other day." This time, she stepped closer, bridging the gap between their yearning bodies. She stepped right into his arms and pressed herself against him as his hands slipped around her waist and shoulders, drawing her close.

"Mari..." He whispered her name with need in his voice as she raised her lips to his.

The kiss was uncontainable. She felt the strength of his arms, the passion in his embrace and the undeniable hardness of him pressing against her. It was intoxicating. *He* was intoxicating. As he always had been. She was swept away as he walked her two steps backward until her calves came in contact with the edge of the bed.

When he eased her downward, she didn't demur. She wanted every second, every moment she could grab in his arms. His tongue worshiped her, sweeping into her mouth in stark possession. His hands caressed her, carrying her down to the bed as gently as his passion would allow.

When the kiss ended, he only took her deeper, settling over her on the bed that was barely big enough for the two of them. Her legs parted, cradling his hips and she despaired of the fabric that lay between them. She wanted to feel the rough skin of his thighs, the smooth, muscled contours of his abs and buttocks under her hands, the way she remembered.

His lips trailed kisses down her neck and onto the small expanse of skin accessible in the vee neck of her shirt. Then the nuisance became too much and she tugged at the hem of her top, wanting it gone. He helped, pulling it off over her head and throwing it aside. He made short work of the front clasp on her bra and then her breasts were in his big hands, her nipples kissed by his possessive lips, then licked, then sucked in the most delicious way. Simon had always known how to touch her, from the first time they'd been together.

They'd made love many times in the comparatively few short weeks they'd been together, but each time had been special and unique. Simon was an inventive lover and the most satisfying of any of the men she had bedded in her admittedly limited experience. She hadn't been able to bear another man's touch since he had left. She hadn't dated, she hadn't even flirted. She'd felt no desire to attract any other man's attention and worried that she would end up alone with only memories of Simon to comfort her in her old age.

That could still happen. In fact, it was more likely now than ever. Simon hadn't said anything about wanting to get back together. He'd told her why he'd left and that reason seemed to continue to plague him. There were too many questions surrounding the future to know what it might hold for the two of them.

But none of that mattered now. Not with Simon's knowing hands on her body, lowering the zipper on her jeans and sliding inside her panties. No, when Simon touched her, all coherent thought slipped from her mind.

She pushed at his shirt, hearing the sound of tearing fabric as she struggled with his clothing. He slid her jeans down her legs along with her panties and then his capable hands took over the task of removing his own clothes. Thank heavens. Within moments, he was as bare as she, lying over her, his muscular thighs in the space between her legs, his cock hard and waiting only for her to be ready to take him.

Simon always sought her pleasure before his own. He was a considerate and expert lover and even in their haste to come together after so long apart, he was careful of her. His hands stroked down over her rib cage as he watched her reactions, then into the vee of her thighs, spreading, parting. His fingers dipped within the wet folds, teasing and making her squirm.

"Don't make me wait, Simon. I need you now!"

"This is going to be so good. Let me make it good for you, Mari." He slid one thick finger into her core, his thumb circling her clit, heightening her pleasure. Bending over her, he placed licking kisses up her abdomen, pausing at her breasts to suck and nibble gently, all the while stroking into her depths with that maddening finger.

"Are you close, sweetheart? Are you going to come?"

"Simon!" She panted, raising her head to watch him as he teased her. He had kept her on the knife's edge of pleasure before but she couldn't take that kind of play tonight. She wanted him more than she'd ever wanted him before. She had to have him.

"That close, eh?" His knowing grin was almost her undoing. "Come for me then, baby. Come on my hand."

As if in response to his wicked words, her inner core clenched hard on his invading fingers. She cried out at the climax that hit her from out of nowhere. It had been fast and not nearly satisfying enough. With Simon though, she knew there was more to come. Only with Simon had she ever achieved multiple orgasms and this promised to be one of those encounters.

He held her gaze as her body quaked around his hand. She was so open to him, so willing to give him everything, anything he asked. She knew it was written all over her face but only his glittering eyes told her how much he hungered for her at that moment, how much he wanted to be inside her. He removed his hand from her body and reached over to grab his pants off the floor.

She followed his movements, glad to see at least one of them was still thinking clearly. Simon grabbed a condom out of his pants pocket, opened the foil packet, and rolled it over himself with efficient movements. Only the slight trembling of his hands told her how much he wanted to be inside her. As much as she wanted him, she guessed.

When he came back to her, she made room for him between her legs and he grinned. An unguarded, sexy grin that took her breath away and made her insides clench.

"I've been dreaming about this, Mari. So many dreams," he whispered. Levering himself into just the right position, he held her gaze as he slid into her.

For Simon, it was like coming home after an eternity away. Her wet heat surrounded him, gloved him in her warmth, like no other woman had ever done. There hadn't been anyone since Mariana, and with all that had happened to him in the interim, he very much doubted any other woman could ever take her place.

She would never know that, of course. He couldn't tell her. It was bad enough he had succumbed now, when she was still in danger from the creatures he hunted. By all rights, he should have left her alone, but circumstances had conspired to bring them together one last time. One last time to hold her, to worship her body with his own and feel…complete.

Simon paused deep within her, savoring the feeling. The forbidden feeling of being one with the only woman who had ever really mattered to him. He wouldn't call it love, thought it was something just as big and scary. She completed him in a way no one else ever had. She was funny, smart, and so beautiful. He cared for her more deeply than he had ever cared for anyone.

Pain lanced through his heart as he thought of having to leave her. Again. For inevitably, he would have to go. He would have to let her get on with her life.

But not today. No, today was a moment out of time. A moment for them to steal. A moment for him to spend making love with the most magical woman he'd ever met.

Simon began to move, each thrust rocking his world. Making love with Mari had always been like that, from the very beginning. It was good to see that hadn't changed in the months since they'd been together last.

"You're beautiful, baby. And so tight. Damn." He tried to hold on to his excitement but it was slipping through his fingers. This first time was going to be fast. He only prayed Mari was with him. He didn't know if he could wait for her this time. It had been too long. Much too long.

"Simon!" She breathed in excited gasps, the evidence of her renewed arousal pushing his own higher. "Simon, I'm so close." She grasped his hips and urged him to move faster, wrapping her luscious legs around him. Little keening moans issued from her lips with his every thrust. He remembered the signs. Thank God, she was as close to oblivion as he was.

Able to let go at last, Simon pounded into her, giving her the slightly rough fuck that he knew she liked. He liked it, too. Almost too much. He had never been able to completely let go like this with another woman. Mari was like no one else. She matched him in every way. Her heels locked around the small of his back, her body stretching beautifully to accommodate him as if she were made to take him, made to receive his passion.

And perhaps she was. There was no doubt he had never found a more perfect bed partner. If he was the type to believe in happily ever after, he would certainly put Mariana at the top of his very short list of possible life mates. In fact, she was the only one on his list.

If he believed in that sort of thing.

But all of that didn't matter as he felt his climax building, ready to release. He touched her, to be certain she would be with him at the last. He wanted her with him…always.

That crazy thought haunting his mind, Simon's orgasm hit him like a fifty-caliber round, punching him skyward in a blinding rush of light and pleasure so intense, he nearly blacked out. He heard her cry out under him and knew she had found the same shuddering release as he spasmed within her tight depths.

She was magic, pure and simple. His Mari. His love.

They spent the day in bed, sleeping only to wake and make love again and again. Mariana had given herself permission to enjoy this time without worrying about the future. It was the only way she could deal with this whole messed-up situation.

Zombies running around in the woods. Simon, back in her life, in her bed. It was all too bizarre and almost too much to take in.

They'd moved to her bedroom in the afterglow of their

first climax together in months. Her bed was bigger and more comfortable than the one in the spare room. Simon had carried her in his arms from the spare room to her room and planted her in her big, fluffy bed. Then they'd lazed there all day, making love and chatting about commonplace things when they weren't dozing in each other's arms. Those were hours out of time, floating in some utopian world.

She had gone into the kitchen once or twice to get them sustenance, but other than that, they'd either been sleeping or making love since sunrise. By sunset, she was sore in places that hadn't been sore since Simon left, and in desperate need of a shower. She soaked in the hot stream of water until Simon came in to fish her out.

That led to a slippery encounter in the shower that almost landed them both on their backsides. Simon's sheer brute strength saved them from more than one potential fall that could have cracked both the porcelain bathroom fixtures and Mari's bones. She was also delighted to discover his inventiveness was back in full force. He had taken her in every position she could think of and a few she had never even contemplated throughout the day. She'd loved every minute of his possession, his passion, his desire.

Only one thing was missing, as it had been during their halcyon days of their past relationship. He had never uttered those three little words she longed to hear. She'd always thought and hoped he had felt the same way about her as she had about him, but he'd never said it in so many words. Mariana thought she'd be beyond the need to hear it now, yet the niggling thought remained with her while she dressed and headed for the kitchen where Simon had promised to prepare a meal before he went out on patrol.

They hadn't talked much about anything serious during the day, spending their time either sleeping or making love. All in all, she'd had worse days, but she didn't think she'd ever had better. Her body was deliciously sore and even with her mind in a whirl, she was looking forward to spending as much time with Simon as she could…before he left her again.

She resolved not to think about that now. She might be deluding herself, but she wanted whatever time she could get with him. For however long it lasted.

Entering the kitchen, she saw he had pulled out all the stops. Chicken breasts from her freezer had been thawed and marinated and were now cooking nicely on the stove. He had made rice and green beans, too. He was fairly well domesticated for a man. Of course, special ops guys were trained to survive in many different kinds of situations. The kitchen training though, had to have come from his mother, or some other nurturing influence in his life. This was too much like a family dinner not to have been something from out of his past.

"Where'd you learn to cook?"

He turned, spatula in hand, and leaned down to give her a quick kiss. Before it could turn into something more, she scooted away from the stove.

"Now is that any way to greet your chef?" He shook the spatula at her in mock chastisement, then turned back to turn the chicken.

"If I let you *greet* me any more, our dinner would end up burnt to a crisp."

He tilted his head as if considering. "You may have a point there."

"So where did you learn to cook like this? It looks and smells wonderful."

"My mother believed her boys should at least know their way around a kitchen. As it happened, I enjoyed helping her. More than my brothers, at least."

This was the first time he had talked about his family with her. When they'd been together before, he'd been very reticent. He had never talked about his past or where he'd come from beyond the basic vital statistics. Something had subtly changed within him in the months since.

It wasn't noticeable at first glance. Only now that some of the barriers between them had broken down, little by little, she was seeing new facets to him that hadn't been visible before. Anytime she had tried to ask about his past before, he'd managed to steer the conversation back to her. He probably knew more about her family than anyone except maybe her family members themselves. He was as adept at evading questions as he was at evading the enemy.

"How many brothers do you have?"

"Two. One older and one younger. All three of us can cook if we have to, but Jeremy and Bobby don't enjoy it half as much as I do. They used to joke that I should become a chef and wear one of those poufy white hats. Then I'd pound some sense into their heads and they'd drop the subject. I still like to cook when I get a chance."

"Lucky me." She smiled at him as he plated the chicken and brought it to the table. He'd already set out the steaming rice and green beans. It was a simple and hearty dinner that both looked and smelled delicious.

"Did they join the military, too?" They served themselves and began to eat.

"I followed Jeremy in, but he went in for jets in a big way. He's a test pilot now, the crazy bastard. Bobby got accepted to Annapolis and is on the fast track to the admiralty if my mother is to be believed. The family is really proud of him. He was always a smart, sort of nerdy kid, and he's grown into a fine officer."

"He's still in?"

Simon nodded as he ate a bite of chicken. "Stationed at the Pentagon right now."

"This is really delicious, by the way. Thanks for cooking. I don't think a man has ever cooked dinner for me before. It's nice."

"Just my way of saying thanks. For letting me stay here and for this afternoon." His expression shuttered. "Mari, I—"

"Don't." She cut him off, unwilling to hear him say it had all been some kind of big mistake. "Let's just say it was for old time's sake and leave it at that."

An uncomfortable silence greeted her words. Not daring

to look at him, she applied herself to her dinner and refused to meet his eyes. She was afraid of what she might find there.

"It was more than just old time's sake, Mari." His low words forced her gaze upward to meet his. His eyes glittered with something she didn't know how to interpret. Strange, when she'd thought she'd known every nuance of his subtle communication. "Thank you for today."

It sounded so formal. She didn't really know what to say, so she nodded tightly and returned her attention to her plate.

"Are you going back out tonight?" She already knew the answer, but desperately needed to change the subject.

"I hunt every night, and will continue to do so until this is finally over."

"It won't be long now though, right? I mean, you said you thought there weren't too many left."

"There were probably about six left, near as we can figure. I got three last night, so that leaves three more. Once they're accounted for, I'll patrol for a few more nights, just to be certain. Then my job will be done."

"And then you'll leave."

"Then I'll leave," he agreed.

"Where will you go? You're not military anymore, so where do you go between assignments?"

"I have a place in southeastern Pennsylvania, near my folks. It's a small farm, actually. I don't have any livestock for it yet. That's in the works. As soon as I get some time to set things up the way I want them, I figured I'd keep a horse or two, maybe some chickens. Later, when I'm not working for hire anymore."

"Sounds like heaven."

"Your dad owned a big spread in Kansas, didn't he?"

"Yeah, I grew up on the farm. It belongs to my brothers now." She was surprised he'd remembered, but then, he had managed to get her entire life's story out of her back when they had been dating.

"You sound like you miss it."

"I didn't think I would, but as I get older, I find myself

longing for the simple things. A little place to plant a vegetable garden and live in peace with nature sounds like heaven to me now."

"What about your medical practice? I thought you wanted the bright lights and the big city after your stint in the Navy was up."

"I guess I did at one time, although I thought I'd stay in the service a lot longer. Things changed as I got older and my priorities realigned. My time in the Navy is almost over. I didn't re-up. I'll be a civilian again in just a few short weeks." She was surprised to hear the almost wistful tone in her voice. "I've been thinking about my options a lot. I've had enough of the hustle and bustle while I was in the Navy. It wasn't what I really thought it would be when I was younger. Now a quiet life appeals to me much more. That's why I opted for this cabin way out here in the woods rather than stay on base or in town. I like the quiet."

"That's quite a change from the way you used to talk." He sat back, finished with his meal, and just watched her.

She shrugged, uncomfortable with his scrutiny. "I've changed in the past few months. My priorities have shifted a bit. That's all."

Unspoken went the thought that the failure of her relationship with him had changed her on a basic level. His leaving and his lack of communication after had made her rethink her priorities in a big way. She had spent a lot of time reevaluating her life and her goals. What had seemed so important when she was younger wasn't nearly as crucial now. No, now the things she had shunned when she left the farm were what mattered most. Family, familiar surroundings, a home to nest in and make her own…and love.

She didn't know if she'd ever really find it, but she wouldn't give up hoping that somehow, she would have love in her life. The love of family, of friends, and if she was really lucky…the love of one special man.

The man sitting across the table from her right now, in fact.

But he was a tough nut to crack. She'd tried, and he'd left. She didn't think she had a chance to convince him now. It was probably too late for them to start over. She would have to settle for what she could get now, because the day spent in his arms had only brought home how much her feelings were still engaged. She loved him with all her heart.

CHAPTER 5

Simon went out the door after a lingering kiss. He had made her promise to stay inside and he'd also left the specially loaded dart pistol with her again, just in case. As the night deepened, so did her fear for both his safety and of the creatures that stalked the night with him, evading and possibly lying in wait for him.

She wasn't foolish enough to go out there, thinking she could be some sort of GI Jane with guns blazing by his side. She knew her limitations, and while she could defend herself if necessary, she was nobody's idea of a warrior. She could hit what she aimed at and had passed the required self-defense tests, but she was a doctor first and foremost. Her calling was to heal, not to tear apart.

And if Simon was to be believed, those fallen Marines out there were really into tearing people apart and sentencing them to join their sinister brotherhood. The thought sent chills down her spine.

Around four in the morning, Mariana heard a noise outside and peeked out the windows to see if she could see anything. Sure enough, in back of the house, she caught a glimpse of light fabric as someone walked through the woods.

The Marines wore camo or dark green. The figure she saw looked small, possibly female. Could it be little Becky Sue McGillicuddy, the twenty-something girl who lived just over the hill with her elderly grandmother?

If so, the girl was in big trouble. The locals had most definitely not been warned about the danger in the woods. It was unusual to see the girl walking alone this early in the morning, but then, Becky Sue had always struck Mariana as a little odd on the few occasions they did chance to meet.

She had to be warned.

Gathering her courage, Mariana opened the back door and stepped onto the porch. Simon's specially loaded pistol was in her hand and her heart was in her throat. She could see more clearly now and it was the girl from the neighboring house, walking calmly along the edge of the trees.

"Becky Sue!" She whispered loudly, hoping to get the girl's attention.

It must not have been loud enough because Becky Sue kept walking at a steady pace, looking neither left nor right. Her path took her nearer to Mariana's house, but the girl was still in the woods, walking almost parallel to Mariana's backyard.

"Becky Sue." She tried again, louder this time.

The girl paused and slowly turned.

Half her face was missing.

Mariana jumped back, her raised hand hitting the frame of the doorway in her haste. She held on to the pistol out of sheer desperation. Becky Sue was one of them. She wasn't *in* danger. She *was* the danger.

The girl changed paths and began walking directly toward Mariana. She didn't hurry. She didn't run. She just walked relentlessly closer as Mariana trembled in fear.

She raised the gun, knowing what she had to do. Now she fully understood Simon's dilemma. Could she shoot a young girl who'd had her whole life ahead of her?

As a doctor, Mariana had dedicated her life to helping people. She had never deliberately shot at someone, even with a dart gun. Especially not a dart gun loaded with a highly dangerous top secret toxin that had to be kept under lock and key. Mariana's hand shook as she took aim. She had to steady both the gun and her nerves. Becky Sue got closer and Mariana could see her more clearly with every step.

She realized she couldn't kill the girl. Becky Sue was already dead. Nobody could survive the kind of injuries she displayed and her pale skin appeared to be completely bloodless. She was a zombie. Like something out of a horror movie.

Praying silently, Mariana pulled the trigger.

A dart flew from the business end of the pistol and landed square in Becky Sue's chest. She didn't even flinch, just kept coming. No pain at all registered on what was left of her once lovely face.

Mariana fired again. The dart hit lower, in Becky Sue's abdomen. She was closer now, out of the tree line and halfway across the grassy yard. A sound traveled on the wind. It was an eerie kind of high pitched moan that sent shivers down Mariana's spine.

She fired once more, backing into the doorway already planning her next move. She would slam the door shut and call Simon's cell number. If he was nearby, he would come help her. The third dart hit Becky Sue midthigh and her steps slowed. The shock of pain was still missing from her ruined face, but her eyes looked queer for just a moment, then she…disintegrated.

She melted from the top down. In less than sixty seconds, she disappeared. All that was left was a dark pile of…something…in Mariana's backyard. She wasn't about to go out to see exactly what it was. Whether the girl had been turned to dust or goo was really beside the point. The toxin had done its job and the once vibrant young girl was now gone forever.

Mariana felt awful about what she'd had to do, yet breathed a huge sigh of relief. She looked around at the woods in case there were any more of them, and seeing none, shut the door, locking it tight behind her. She was safe for now.

She said a prayer for poor Becky Sue McGillicuddy, and one for Simon while she was at it. Now more than ever, she understood how hard this mission was for him. He wasn't made of stone, no matter what anyone thought. He had a compassionate heart under all that macho bravado. He had to feel something for those fallen soldiers he had to lay to rest. He had to have some feelings about the experiment gone so terribly wrong for those first fallen comrades, and for the later victims, and the horrific way they had died.

Mariana touched her face, not really surprised to find tears running down her cheeks. She felt sick to her stomach, but muscled through, ignoring the nausea as best she could, keeping vigilant watch on the woods from the corners of her windows. If there were any more of them out there, she now knew what to expect. Of course, Becky Sue hadn't been a highly trained soldier in life. The others, if they truly retained some of their life's skills, would be much harder to deal with than the innocent young girl from down the road.

Although she kept watch until dawn, no more of the nightmare creatures came to call. Simon marched in from the tree line as the sun rose fully, looking tired. He paused at the pile of rubbish that used to be Becky Sue McGillicuddy and his jaw tightened. After a moment, he continued toward Mariana's back porch, a little more energy in his step.

Mariana flung open the door and reached for him as he climbed her back steps.

"Thank heaven you're all right." She kissed his stubbly cheek, then his waiting lips.

"What's this? You're shaking. And what was that I saw in your yard?" He held her away from him, his expression grim.

"That was Becky Sue, from next door. I saw her in the woods around four this morning and tried to warn her, but…" Her gaze trailed to the lump of dirty clothing and organic debris in her yard. "Simon, half her face was missing. I used the darts you left but she didn't go down right away. I fired three times. Hit her three times. It seemed to take forever. Just when I was going into panic mode, she…dissolved. Melted, right in front of my eyes."

Simon tugged her into his chest, placing one big hand on her hair as he hugged her, offering comfort. He felt so good. Whole and unharmed by the terrors of the night. He was her rock of comfort in a sea of confusion. Her body trembled in remembered fear and he calmed her with gentle touches.

Somehow, he had walked her inside and kicked the door shut behind them. She didn't remember him doing it, but she felt the play of his muscles when he reached behind his back to lock the dead bolt on the back door. He maneuvered her toward a kitchen chair and helped her sit.

"I'm going to make you some coffee. Okay?" She nodded as he moved toward the automatic coffeemaker. He put the water in and added more grounds than she normally used to the filter cup, then switched the thing on and turned back to her. The sound of perking and the strong scent of brewing coffee filled the small kitchen within moments. It felt oddly comforting. Commonplace and routine, it brought sanity back to her life faster than she would have believed possible.

Simon leaned against the kitchen counter and regarded her with concern. "Better now?" She nodded again. "You'll be steadier once you get some coffee in you. Now, tell me about this neighbor. Does she live alone?"

"Oh, no." She realized what he was getting at. If Becky Sue had been attacked, more than likely, so had the sweet little old lady that was her grandmother.

Simon cursed and turned to the coffeepot, removing the carafe and filling a mug directly from the stream of freshly brewed coffee. When it was half full, he replaced the carafe and handed the mug to her.

"Drink this. It'll perk you up and steady your nerves." She did as ordered, though she usually didn't go for such strong, black coffee. "I take it from your reaction, the girl didn't live alone?"

Mariana clung to the mug for strength even as the strong

brew started to permeate her body. Surprisingly, it helped her focus as the caffeine hit her system.

"She lived with her grandmother. Just the two of them."

Simon's expression grew even grimmer. "How close is their place?"

"Just over the hill. They're my nearest neighbors."

"I know the house. I've scouted it before. Damn." He filled a cup for himself from the coffee maker. "How old is the grandmother? Can she get around okay?"

"She's pretty old and suffers from arthritis. Becky Sue pretty much took care of her. I visited them once or twice, but they mostly kept to themselves."

"I'll need to go check on the grandmother and their house."

"You don't think…" Her words trailed off when he turned to her. She could see he did indeed think the worst. "If she was crippled in life and unable to get around much, would she still be that way under the influence of this contagion?"

"I truly have no idea. The only people I've seen infected were fit young Marines. But I guess I'm going to find out."

"I'm going with you. If she wasn't infected, she'll be frightened and may need help. There's no way of knowing how long ago Becky Sue was attacked. Her grandmother could have been alone for days. She'll be disoriented and frightened if you show up on her doorstep. At least she knows me, if only in passing. Plus, I'm a doctor. Mrs. McGillicuddy knows that." Simon seemed unconvinced by her argument. "It's daylight and it's supposed to be sunny all day. Didn't you tell me the others hide from the sun? It should be safe to take a quick drive over to their house, check things out, and come back. It'll only take a few minutes, and you'll be with me the entire time, right? What could go wrong?"

Grim faced, Simon relented. "All right, but we do this my way. I'll approach the house first and check things out. If the old lady is still alive, I'll signal you in. If not, you stay clear.

Got it?"

"Aye, aye, sir." She gave him a salute and a smile, glad to see his expression soften just the tiniest bit.

"Take the pistol with you. How many rounds do you have left?"

Mariana checked the specially crafted handgun. It could hold up to six dart rounds in an oversized, rotating cylinder. She'd only used three on Becky Sue.

"Three left. How many does it usually take to disintegrate one of those creatures?"

Some of the grimness returned to his eyes. "Theoretically, it should only take one, or so the experts tell me. As you probably saw, I've learned it actually takes awhile for the toxin to spread and do its work. Multiple rounds help the process along. I usually use at least two if possible—one in the upper body and one in the lower. The key is to hit them while they're still some distance away, or when you're in a position to retreat quickly to a safe distance."

"Good to know." She hated to think how hard won his knowledge was.

"Finish up your coffee and we'll get on the road. I want to do this, then report in before I go down for the day." He rubbed his unshaven face in a rare outward show of fatigue. He was unbending more and more around her, showing that he was, indeed human, after all. That was something he had never really done during their previous involvement.

"How'd you do last night?" She watched his expression as she sipped the strong coffee.

"I got two more. By our counts, there should be only one left, but if they've infected civilians, the problem has spread."

"That's not good," she observed, stating the obvious.

"No, not good at all." He swallowed the last of his coffee and placed his mug in the sink.

She grabbed her jacket, stowed the pistol within easy reach in one pocket, and headed for the front door, next to which was her car, a small, sturdy SUV. Simon said nothing when she made for the driver's seat, though he did open her door for her as soon as she chirped the locks open. He was a gentleman, after all.

She noticed him looking into the back before opening the door, probably checking to be certain the spacious vehicle was indeed empty before they got in. She would have to remember to do that herself. She wasn't used to living under near constant threat. Until this situation was fully resolved, she would have to be more cautious.

"I meant to tell you before," he said as he got in on the passenger's side and shut the door. "I like your choice of vehicle. My little brother has one of these and I borrowed it the last time I moved. It holds a lot more than I expected."

She guessed he was making small talk as a way to defuse her fear. It wasn't working, but she loved him for trying. She was wound tighter than a top and wouldn't rest until they knew one way or the other if that sweet, crippled old woman had been attacked by something out of a nightmare.

"I appreciate what you're trying to do." She turned to look at him as she started the car.

"What?"

"Come on, Simon. You're not exactly the chatty type. Thank you for trying to take my mind off it, but I'll never forget what I saw—what I did—tonight."

"And you never should," Simon agreed, surprising her. "If it helps, try to remember that girl was already dead. You helped put her soul to rest. You didn't kill her. She was dead a long time before the creature she'd become tried to attack and kill you. It was both self-defense and an act of mercy."

"Will the courts see it that way?" A dreadful thought entered her mind. "Simon, I never even thought about the legal ramifications of this. Becky Sue was a civilian. Do we have the right to do what I did to civilians? What about the law?"

"I'm operating under the highest authority, Mari. Orders from the president himself, cosigned by the director of the Centers for Disease Control. This contagion has to be stopped at all costs and I'm authorized to use any and all means necessary to end it wherever it spreads, be it to military or civilian personnel. When I make my report to Commander Sykes tonight, I'm going to mention the continued problems you've had on your land, but otherwise I'm keeping you out of this, Mari. They'll know you're aware of the contagion and the creatures. That's it. Anything else, let it be on my head."

"But Simon—"

"No. Trust me on this. Everything surrounding this experiment has been screwed up from day one. I don't want your name all over some top secret dossier somewhere. It's bad enough that as it is, you'll be a footnote in the file. I don't want this to come back to haunt you at a later date." His jaw set in a stubborn line even as his words struck fear in her heart.

"Do you expect more trouble?"

"Honey, I always expect trouble. It's the only thing that's kept me alive this long." He let out a heavy sigh, his stance relenting just a bit. "I've been walking a tightrope here. They know I'm immune. Already the research team wants to know why. I only have Matt Sykes to thank for the fact that the researchers don't know my name or how to find me. I trust Matt. After this is over, I'm going to fade away where those mad scientists will never find me."

"But won't they know who did the job of cleaning up the base?"

"That's where the mercs come in. All the paperwork is run through them. Some creative paper shuffling should keep my name far from Quantico for many moons to come." He shrugged. "It helps to have friends in interesting places. As for you, I want any record of your involvement as limited as we can make it. The locations of all the kills are being recorded by the cleanup team. There's no way around that. They'll know about the action on your land. You'll be listed as a witness in the reports. That's as far as I want it to go."

She was uncomfortable with the idea of lying, even by omission. Simon was so serious though, he convinced her of the need for secrecy. And really, what could it hurt for the reports to say Simon took the shots that disintegrated poor Becky Sue? Mariana would always know the truth. She would always remember what she'd done.

"So what about the McGillicuddys? Becky Sue, and possibly her grandmother? How will their disappearance be explained? People do check on them and visit from time to time."

"When I call Matt, he'll help square it. He's good at that sort of thing. I imagine there'll be some sort of cover-up to explain the girl's disappearance and satisfy the locals. Don't worry." He reached out to take her hand. "I won't let anything bad happen to you. I promise."

The seriousness of his vow took her by surprise. She had known he cared on some level, but what she saw in his expression—more open to her now than he had ever been before—floored her. He'd never made her any promises before. This could be a breakthrough moment, if she was foolish enough to believe he would let her into his life after this crisis was over.

Only time would tell.

She squeezed his hand and gave him a sad smile. "Thank you, Simon. That means a lot to me."

"Mari," he tugged on her hand, leaning over the small console to meet her lips in a soft, gentle kiss. "You mean a lot to me. I never told you before, but I don't think I could survive if something happened to you on my watch."

Simon kissed her once more and let go, turning away to gaze out the window. He'd almost revealed too much there. The sad, scared look on her beautiful face had made him want to ease her hurt and fear. She had looked so lost. It tugged on his heart and made him want to comfort her.

If the situation wasn't so urgent, he would march her right back into the house and make love to her until her eyes lost that shadow of apprehension. She was dealing well with a situation in which she was totally out of her depth. He was damned proud of her, but he also wanted to protect her.

Make her go back into her house and batten down the hatches until it was safe again. Or better yet, go get a room on base until the terror was over. He wanted her safe. He wanted her happy. He wanted her. Period.

Mariana put the SUV in gear and headed for the gravel lane that led to the neighboring house. He had done reconnaissance on the entire area and was familiar with the layout of each house and outbuilding where the creatures might possibly try to hide. He had found more than one making use of someone's garden shed in the first few weeks. After he'd dispatched those, the others seemed to have steered clear of such places. They apparently had the capacity to learn from mistakes, which made them even tougher to deal with in the long run.

The one Marine that was left was one he'd been hunting for a long time. This one had been part of a sniper-spotter team. He had been an expert at stealth in life and had demonstrated a propensity for the same now that he was…something else. He'd also been one of the original test subjects. He'd died honorably in battle, only to have his body experimented on after death to become a thing of nightmares. Nobody deserved that.

As they made their way down the lane, Simon decided to share a little more information with Mariana. She had already faced two of the creatures, and they might be walking into the lair of a third. She deserved to know what he'd learned and observed during his time in the field hunting these creatures. Plus, it would help him organize his thoughts to bounce them off her. She had always challenged him intellectually, and he respected her knowledge and ability to reason things out.

"They're able to learn simple things." He could tell he had surprised her by speaking. She listened attentively even as she navigated the narrow gravel lane. "Luckily, the more complex operations, like using firearms, seem to be beyond them."

"Thank heaven for that, at least. I can only imagine a platoon of zombie Marines able to use Uncle Sam's artillery against an unsuspecting populace. Talk about a nightmare."

She caught on quick. He really enjoyed that about her. "They can use simple weapons like sticks and such. The knowledge of anything more mechanical than opening a door seems to have disappeared along with their humanity. They don't move fast but they can sneak up on you if you're not careful. They don't talk either. Sometimes they make a sort of moaning sound."

"I heard that when Becky Sue got close. It was horrible. Like she was begging for help or something. I've had a few patients make similar sounds while they were delirious, but Becky Sue's vocalizations sounded like a wounded animal. It was inhuman."

"She *wasn't* human. Not any longer, Mari. Try not to let it get to you. You did the right thing. You put the girl out of her misery and let her soul finally rest in peace."

"I didn't know you had a spiritual side, Simon." She raised one eyebrow in his direction as she slowed the vehicle. They were close to the neighbor's house. He saw no problem with parking in the old lady's drive and knocking on the door. There was bright sunshine in the sky and the zombies shunned the light. If the worst had happened and the old lady had been turned, she should be cowering inside. If she was still alive, she would probably welcome a visit from Mariana after not seeing her granddaughter for a day or two.

Simon shrugged off Mariana's interest in his spiritual beliefs. "Like most soldiers, I have faith in a higher power. I've seen too many weird things and too much death not to believe the spirit lives on."

They arrived at the neighbor's house and Mariana parked in the drive. There was an open space between the car and the house, which suited him just fine. He felt the weight of her stare.

"That's deep," she commented when he finally looked at her.

He had to laugh. His Mari always managed to surprise him with her reactions. She'd managed to take a very serious situation and make it light without discounting the innermost thoughts he'd just revealed.

"Look, I want you to stay here. Keep the car doors locked, and the windows rolled up. I'm going to do some recon around the house. I'll make one circuit of the perimeter and then come back to you. If I don't see anything suspicious, we can go knock on the door together, just in case your neighbor is all right. She would probably be alarmed to see a strange man at her door, but like you said, she knows you. If she's been turned, I'll take care of her. I want you to stand clear. Run back to the car and lock yourself inside. There's still one Marine unaccounted for and he's the smartest of the bunch that I've faced. He could be hiding around here somewhere. Especially if he's the one who attacked Becky Sue."

He hated the fear that reentered her eyes. Unfortunately, she had to know the truth about what they could be facing.

"If you see anything bad while I'm gone, honk the horn. A short tap for something suspicious. Two taps if you see one of them in the distance. Lay on the horn if you need immediate help. I'll come running."

She visibly gulped and he took her hand, leaning in to kiss the fear away. She warmed to him, but this wasn't the time or place. Why couldn't he keep his hands off her? Why couldn't he get enough of her? And why was he tormenting them both this way—letting them both glimpse something that could never be?

No doubt about it, he was a glutton for punishment. Still, his duty was clear. She had been dragged into this mess and he had to stay by her side and protect her until the situation was resolved. He owed her that much at least. He would do the same for anyone, but knowing it was Mari who was in danger made it all that much more disturbing to his psyche, his deeply buried emotions…and his heart.

"Be good while I'm gone." He gave her a lopsided smile as he drew back, liking the way her eyes dilated in pleasure even under such dire circumstances. For that short moment in time, she wasn't scared anymore. He had given her that respite. It made him feel proud and even more protective.

"Be careful, Simon." She touched his sleeve as he opened the car door.

"Don't worry. I do this for a living." He winked at her and slipped out of the SUV, waiting by the door until she locked it behind him. With a parting grin, he left her to do a circuit of the house.

CHAPTER 6

Mariana watched him go with her heart in her throat. She hated seeing him in danger. She knew intellectually that in his profession, he often put himself in harm's way, but actually seeing it—participating in it, even to a small degree—was something very different. Watching every tree branch for movement, she did her best to stay vigilant, biting her lip when the sun dipped behind a scudding cloud for a long minute.

She watched what she could see of the sky through her moon roof. It looked like clouds were gathering, which could mean trouble.

Mariana didn't breathe easy until she saw Simon rounding the corner of the house, moving at ease though obviously alert. He ambled up to the driver's side window and she rolled it down to talk to him.

"It looks clear. Clouds could pose a problem later, but it's still a little too bright for them to be very active. Come on out and let's check on the old lady."

She popped the locks and Simon opened her door for her, his head swiveling to check all directions before he stepped back to let her out. She was careful to chirp the doors locked behind her as she walked at Simon's side up to the front porch. The place looked welcoming, with bright pink petunias in the flower boxes and a profusion of red and white impatiens lining the walk.

There was no sound from within though, which was troubling. Mrs. McGillicuddy couldn't get around much, but she loved her television. From sunrise to sunset that old TV was usually blaring some game show or soap opera. Now it was eerily silent.

She looked up at Simon with apprehension. "Something's wrong. She usually has the TV turned up loud all day long."

Simon immediately took point. "Stay behind me. I'll knock, you get ready to run if this goes bad."

She nodded, knowing he was the only one who could really face these monsters. He had already been bitten and lived to tell the tale. Nobody else had been so lucky. It was likely she would face the same fate as Becky Sue if she got stupid and got bitten.

Simon walked up to the door and knocked loudly. "Call out to her," he instructed.

"Mrs. McGillicuddy. It's Mariana, from next door. I came to see if you were all right." She spoke as loudly as she could, given the lump in her throat. "Mrs. McGillicuddy, are you there, ma'am?"

A shuffling sound came from within the house and then she heard that distinctive, inhuman moaning sound. The sun was swallowed for the moment by a thick cloud, casting a pall over the landscape. Mariana cringed, shuddering as she realized her worst fears had come true. Becky Sue's grandmother—that sweet, crippled old lady—had been turned into a zombie.

"Get back to the car. I'll handle it." Simon's words were clipped as he braced himself to kick in the old wooden door. "Stay alert. There could be more. Run. Now!"

She pulled out the pistol and held it ready as she flew back down the porch steps, looking wildly all around as she made a beeline for her SUV. Behind her she heard an ominous crack as Simon broke through the door with one solid kick. Then she heard the faint report of the rifle as he shot twice in quick succession. His boots hit the wooden boards of the porch steps with loud, hurried steps as she unlocked her car door. She pushed inside, barely remembering to check the backseat before she got in and locked the doors tight.

Turning, she watched in horror as poor old Mrs. McGillicuddy made her way down her porch steps. The plump old lady was walking stiffly and her head looked misshapen. Mariana realized why as she drew closer. Her skull had been bashed in and it looked like something—or someone—had been gnawing on her brain.

Mariana had to stifle the urge to vomit. She had seen a lot of things as a doctor but never anything as truly horrific as this.

Simon reached the car and she unlocked the passenger side door for him. He hopped inside with little fanfare and slammed the door shut.

"Back up to the end of the lane. She should go any second now."

Mariana didn't have to be told twice. The gruesome specter of Mrs. McGillicuddy advanced steadily, the flailing ends of Simon's darts sticking out of her neck and hip. He'd hit cleanly and if their luck held, she would disintegrate any minute now.

Mariana backed the SUV to the end of the gravel drive and waited. The old woman advanced a few more steps, reaching out as if for help, making that high pitched moaning sound. But there was nothing more they could do for the poor old thing.

Mrs. McGillicuddy took one more step and then began to dissolve, melting from the sites of the darts, inward. It was all over in a matter of seconds. Mariana gripped her steering wheel, shaken to the core. It was one thing to see it happen in the dark of night. It was quite another to watch a sweet old lady turned monster melt before her eyes in the harsh light of day.

"Sweet Lord," she whispered.

Simon's hand on her thigh snapped her attention to him. "It's better this way, Mari."

"I know you're right, but... *Damn*, Si. This isn't something they prepared me for in medical school, or even in boot camp. This is a nightmare come to life."

"Welcome to my world. I've been living with this for months now. I'm only sorry you got dragged into it." He removed his hand and turned to scan the trees. "The only good thing is that it will all be over soon."

"But it's spread to civilians."

"Yeah, that is a problem. Luckily, there are only the two houses in this area—this one, and yours. You're safe, and the two occupants of this place are now accounted for. With any luck, it hasn't spread any further. Now if I can just get that last Marine, we can call this done. Frankly, it'll be a relief."

"I can understand that." Yes, she understood it, but feared the end of his mission would spell the end of their renewed affair. It was an agonizing thought. She wasn't ready to give him up yet.

"Drive back up to the old lady's house. I have to check inside, to make sure she was alone."

She hated the thought of him going back in there, but knew he had to be certain. This contagion was too dangerous to allow to spread any further. She pulled up next to the house again and left the car running. If they had to make a quick escape, she would be ready.

"Remember the signal?"

"Tap my horn once for something suspicious. Twice if I see one of them far away. Lean on it if I've got a serious problem."

"Good girl." He smiled as he leaned close to give her a peck on the cheek.

Simon was out of the car and in the house before she could tell him to be careful again. She watched the surroundings, her eyes straying to the destroyed front door of the house every few seconds, willing Simon to reappear, safe and sound.

She thought she saw something flicker through the woods, but wasn't certain enough to sound the horn. A few minutes later, Simon appeared at the door. His expression was closed as usual. There was no real urgency in his movements, which she took as a very good sign. Likely, the rest of the house was clear.

He made a few hand signals that she interpreted to mean he was going to scout the grounds again. He disappeared around the side of the house and she went back to waiting. If this is what his life was like in the special forces, he could keep it. Moments of blind panic interspersed with what felt like hours of tense waiting. All in all, her medical job was easier on the nerves. Even her stint in the Emergency Room a few years back had been less nerve wracking than this.

Simon appeared again a few minutes later. He stopped by the pile of debris that had been Mrs. McGillicuddy and dropped a small object onto the ground. He gave the area another searching look, then ambled up to the passenger side door. She unlocked it for him and he climbed in. She could see the weariness of the long night in every move of his muscular body. The man needed sleep and a few hours away from the tension of his mission.

"As your doctor, I'm prescribing bed rest for the next six hours, at least." She always enjoyed the challenge of making him smile and was rewarded when one side of his lips quirked upward.

"I'll be glad to follow your orders, ma'am, as soon as I report in. Commander Sykes has to get the cleanup team to sanitize this area as well as your backyard ASAP. It's standard operating procedure for this mission sent down from the CDC. I mark all the kill sites and the hazmat guys come in and do their thing. You didn't see them, but they were out behind your house yesterday."

"When?" She was shocked by the idea that a group of soldiers had been on her property and she'd never even known about it.

"When I was keeping you otherwise occupied." His eyes

heated with remembered desire and her stomach clenched.

"Damn, Simon. Is that what had you so eager to keep me in bed all day?" She put the SUV in gear and backed out of the driveway again, turning onto the gravel road.

"No, sweetheart, that was just a fringe benefit. I didn't want you worrying."

"So what changed?" She began the short drive back to her place.

"The girl was bad enough, but now her grandmother. You're involved now, Mari, more than you should be. I didn't want you in this at all, but you're in it now, up to your neck. You have a right to know the full parameters of the op and what happens next. You're a doctor, after all. I bet you were already speculating about what happened to the remains after I did my part of the job. Weren't you?"

She shook her head. "You know me too well. I just didn't think you'd tell me so much about the operation, Simon. I know it's probably all top secret, right?"

"It is. And you'll be held to that top secret classification. Which means you don't talk about any of this to anyone except me. You've already seen and done too much to be kept out of the loop. I talked to Matt Sykes last night, while you were in the shower, and he agreed."

"You already talked to Commander Sykes about me?" That was a surprise.

"He needed to know where I've been. He's keeping close tabs on me since I'm the only thing standing between the base, the surrounding populace, and…well…what you saw happen to your neighbors."

She thought about that. "A lot of responsibility is riding on your shoulders, Simon."

"It's what I do." He shrugged. The casual attitude didn't fool her. She knew he was feeling every bit of that responsibility. Simon always took important things, like his duty, very seriously indeed.

She would have said more but a flash of white at the side of the road caught her eye. She slammed on the brakes.

"What?" he asked, instantly alert.

"I thought I saw something." She backed up the SUV carefully. "Look over there." She pointed to a dense patch of greenery. It was ripped up and torn now that she looked closely, with obvious tire tracks leading away from the gravel road bed and onto the dirt and grass at the side of the road.

Simon hefted his weapon and slid out of the vehicle. "Stay here and keep the engine running." She didn't have to be told to lock the doors behind him as her heart crept into her throat yet again.

Simon approached the vehicle. It was small, boxy and white, with the distinctive stripes and logo of the Postal Service. Even from several yards out he could see the smashed windows and deep red streaks of blood all over the interior of the crashed Jeep. Mail was strewn all around, but the postman was nowhere to be seen.

No doubt he'd been attacked and was likely already dead.

Another fatality in a string of deaths that had gone on far too long. And another target to add to his list. Simon dropped a transmitter tag in the vehicle, did a quick sweep of the area, and headed back to Mariana's SUV.

She waited for him with the world in her smile. The relief on her face as he broke from the cover of trees warmed him from the inside out. God, she was good to come home to. These past days had teased him with a glimpse of how good life could be.

But not for him.

He was weakening, though. His resolve to stay detached was on the wane. Would he be strong enough to resist the allure of her? Would he be able to do the right thing when this was all over? Would he have the strength to leave her again? He wasn't so sure. And that thought was even scarier than the zombies.

He didn't want to hurt her. He didn't want to ruin her life. Right now, he was still firmly convinced that his continued presence in her life could only accomplish both of those things. He just didn't see how being with him could spell anything but disaster for her.

For one thing, there was his…affliction, for lack of a better word. He had been changed by the attack on a cellular level. Nobody could tell him for certain what that would mean for him in the long term. For another, there was his job. Although he was no longer at Uncle Sam's beck and call, he was still employed in the same line of work. He had to pick up and go when he got the call. Nowadays he could either accept or pass on jobs, at his discretion. That was different, but if he wanted to get paid, he had to work. It was that simple.

Still, he knew he couldn't do mercenary work forever. At some point he would be too slow to be good in the field and that day grew nearer with every passing moment. Younger, faster guys would take his place in the field, and he would either have to find a new line of work, or find a way to utilize his hard won skills as a training officer or operations manager of some kind. He'd been thinking a lot about it since the attack that had left him in the hospital for weeks. He still hadn't arrived at any conclusive decisions.

Crossing paths with Mariana had started those thoughts of retirement up again in his mind. If he found a less dangerous way to earn a living, could he somehow convince her to share his future? However long that lasted? Would it be fair to her? He still didn't have an answer.

He approached her vehicle, careful to look everywhere before signaling her to pop the locks. He slid into the passenger seat and dreaded giving her the news. She was strong and had been a real trooper up to this point. He hated to lay even more on her, but she needed to know what they were up against, so she would be wary.

"It was a postal vehicle. The driver is gone, probably dead. The claw marks on the sides of the Jeep look like they were made by our target. Probably in the last few hours. It's dark under the trees and the clouds have been hiding the sun off and on."

"Jeff Humbolt is the postman on this route. He lives alone out on Webster Road. You think he's turned into one of them?"

He nodded, thinking through the possibilities. He knew where Webster Road was. It wasn't too far from here, in fact, out near the edge of the woods and very isolated. Up to this point, the zombies hadn't strayed far from this patch of woods, bordering the base. But if the postman retained some affinity for his home area, he might try to make it back home tonight, after the contagion ran its course and he rose from the dead.

"Let's go back to your place. I need to report in and get some sleep. Tonight is soon enough to go after the wayward mailman. The contagion takes awhile to take over its host."

"Poor Jeff. He was a sweet old coot. A widower. He used to flirt with me for fun, not in a serious way." He saw Mariana try to hide a tear as she surreptitiously wiped her cheek.

Simon was touched by the sadness on her face and in her voice as she put the SUV in gear and started off toward her house once more. She had lost people she knew to this horrific contagion and had been attacked and threatened herself. Most women would be a blubbering mess right about now, but not his Mari. No, she was soldiering on, even though he knew she was having a hard time dealing with all of this.

Hell, he had a hard time dealing with it, too. Of course, he'd had a lot longer to get used to the idea of the walking dead. Of zombies running around trying to eat their victims' faces.

"I'm sorry, Mariana."

"It's not your fault, Simon. If anyone's to blame, it's the scientists and doctors who unleashed this thing on an unsuspecting world. My profession has a lot to answer for this time. I hope they came down hard on the person or persons responsible for this tragedy."

"I heard the entire science team was being held

incommunicado pending the resolution of my mission. They were allowed to develop the toxin to stop the zombies, but they've been effectively put into custody awaiting judgment. Someone else is gathering the data on where and when I tracked and killed the creatures. Hopefully a new, more ethical group of doctors will be appointed to figure out what went wrong and how to prevent it from ever happening again."

"I suppose the fact that the original team came up with an effective way to stop their creations will count in their favor." Mari's tone was grudging and he knew she was angry, thinking about her defenseless neighbors and the postman who had been murdered in such a heinous way.

"You could probably testify as to what you saw. It might make a difference when their fates are decided. The proceedings will be top secret, of course. Sykes could get you an interview with counsel, I suppose, if you want to go that far."

"I'll have to think about it. It's not a bad idea. At the very least, I could submit an affidavit of some kind so the judge will know the true extent of the civilian consequences. Someone should speak up for Becky Sue, her grandmother, and Mr. Humbolt, the postman. They didn't deserve to die that way. The people responsible should be made aware of the human consequences of their actions, as should those who will decide their punishment and whether or not they get to practice medicine or conduct experiments in the future."

"It couldn't hurt." Simon admired her desire to see justice done on behalf of her neighbors.

"Can I ask you a question about the zombies' condition? You may not know the answer, but I've been wondering why they have claws. They didn't die that way. Most human beings keep their nails trimmed and they're not that thick."

"Yeah, that surprised me at first too. The geeks tell me it has to do with the contagion's effect on dead tissue. It reanimates it, and with older tissue, it seems to have slight regenerative properties. It makes the nails on both hands and feet thicker and longer. They seem to keep getting longer up to the point where the dead body rises. Once that happens, the contagion has run its course in the host and it doesn't reactivate until it finds a new body to kill, then bring back."

"That's really sinister, when you stop to think about it." She looked appalled, as well she should.

"You can say that again." They pulled into the driveway leading to her cabin. "Those claws threw us all for a loop the first time we saw them. It took the scientists about a week to figure out why that happened to their original test subjects. I've been reporting my observations through Sykes. Even though this experiment is a total bust, at least someone is learning something from it. For one thing, the toxin to destroy the creatures is a brand-new and useful discovery."

"Necessity is the mother of invention yet again, I suppose." Mariana sighed and he knew she was upset by the horrific deaths her unknown colleagues had caused.

They pulled up in front of her house and Simon turned to her.

"Stay put for a minute while I check the perimeter, okay?" He waited for her nod of agreement before he set off. He couldn't be too careful with her safety. She had already been stalked by these creatures twice. That was twice too many times as far as he was concerned. He shuddered to think how he would have felt if she'd been infected and he'd had the grim task of ending her.

He frankly didn't know if he could survive it.

When he was satisfied the perimeter around the cabin was clear, he motioned for her to leave her vehicle. She joined him by the front entry and he continued to scan the area as she unlocked the door.

He went in first, just to be certain the house remained undisturbed since their departure. Everything was as it should be and he ushered her inside, locking the door tight behind them. He breathed easy for the first time that morning.

"I have to call Sykes."

"I'll make a bite for us to eat. I don't know about you, but

I need fuel and then sleep."

"Sounds like the perfect plan." He pulled her close for a quick hug and kissed the top of her head before letting her go. He needed to touch her, to be sure she was really there and really all right. It was a need in his blood that grew stronger with every passing minute.

He went into the living room to make his call while she headed for the kitchen.

CHAPTER 7

Mariana could hear Simon's deep murmuring voice coming from the living room, though she couldn't tell what he was saying. She liked having him in her house. He made her feel safe, even in this horrific situation.

She put together a few sandwiches for them, unwilling and unable to spend a lot of energy on cooking anything more complex at the moment. They needed something to eat and they needed sleep. Both of them had been up all night, and while Mariana had gotten used to pulling all-nighters and double shifts as a young intern, it had been a while since she'd been called upon to stretch her endurance to the limit. She had been running on adrenaline for the past few hours and desperately needed some real, deep, healing sleep.

She figured Simon was only a little better off than she was. While he'd trained himself to run on little to no sleep, at some point the human body needed to crash and recharge. They'd spent all day yesterday sleeping in short snatches between furious bouts of lovemaking. While she felt more relaxed than she had in months, neither of them had really gotten any deep, restorative sleep. They both had to be running on fumes today.

"Sykes is up to date. He's going to send the cleanup team

to the neighbors' house first, then they'll fix up your yard." Simon came into the kitchen and snagged one of the sandwiches she was about to place on a serving platter. He ate half of it before she could even blink an eye.

He took the platter out of her hands and ushered her to the table, setting the plate of sandwiches between them as they both sat. She grabbed a sandwich and ate mechanically, knowing she needed the nutrition but not really tasting the food at all. She was just too tired. She was aware of Simon watching her as the silence dragged. Looking at him, she had to catch her breath at the glitter of emotion in his eyes. There was a mixture of longing, care, and a hint of possession that made her feel oddly cherished.

"Eat up, Mari." He tipped the platter toward her and urged her to take another of the sandwich halves she had prepared. After she took another, he got up and fished two tall glasses out of a cupboard and filled them both with ice cold milk from her refrigerator.

"How did your talk go with the commander?" she asked as he placed one of the glasses in front of her and sat back down.

"He wasn't thrilled that you'd been stalked twice. There will be some top secret paperwork added to your file, and the op file, that will cover you with the brass should they get wind of this operation at some point in the future. For now, everything is being kept need-to-know and will likely remain so for many years to come. Nobody wants a repeat of this. What really concerns me is that if the limited success in my case was known, some moron somewhere would try this again. Only five people know what really happened to me and all the written and electronic records of my treatment have been wiped. It was one of the conditions I put on taking this mission. I didn't want to become a lab rat they would poke at until they figured out how I survived. This thing is just too dangerous."

"Smart thinking." Simon had always been brilliant. He was right to realize that the scientists wouldn't leave him alone if they knew about his survival and his new healing abilities. He was in a dangerous situation, even without the creatures he was hunting. If the wrong kind of person knew what his body could do, he might just be in a world of trouble. "Who are the five people that know about you?"

"Matt Sykes, the civilian doctor, and two nurses that treated me when I was sick, and now you."

"Are you sure you can trust them all?"

"I trust you without question." She liked the way he put her at the head of the list. His trust was something she knew wasn't easily given. "Matt Sykes and I go way back. He's one of my oldest and best friends. He won't betray me. The civilian doctor is an older fellow. After I was bitten, I didn't report it. The op was over and I went to my apartment off base to crash. I don't remember anything until two days later when I dragged myself to a local clinic. I felt too sick to make it to the base hospital, but as it turned out, that was probably the best move for me. The man who runs the clinic, Doctor Shepard, is like an old-fashioned country doctor. He was trained by the best, and moved to the small town outside the base when his oldest boy was killed in action a few years back. He says I remind him of his son. Doc Shepard was the first to point out what a problem I'd have if that science team learned what happened to me. He gave me the original records that would've betrayed anything about my rapid healing, and destroyed the rest. He thought I might need them down the road if something went wrong, but felt nobody else should know unless I wanted them to."

"Sounds like a smart man." Mariana began to think maybe Simon was in the clear—as much as possible—from being turned into a human guinea pig. "Who were the nurses?"

"One was Doctor Shepard's wife, Matilda. The other was Jenny Shepard, the doctor's daughter-in-law. It was her husband who'd been killed in action. I don't think either of those ladies would betray me. They watched over me for weeks in their clinic. After I dragged myself to his office, I pretty much collapsed. He took me in and those women nursed me while I was out of it. I owe them my life."

"You got really lucky, Simon."

"I know. Things could have gone a lot worse for me, especially early on, if the military science team had known what happened. Doctor Shepard helped me clear things with the military doctors. He told them I had pneumonia and I used up all my accumulated leave. I went back, finished the few weeks on my tour, and retired as planned. I contacted Matt Sykes and told him what had happened because I knew he still had a big problem on his hands, and I was the only one who could safely go in and solve it."

"So you volunteered for this duty?" It didn't really surprise her. Simon wasn't the type to sit idle when he knew there was something he could do to help.

"I knew if they sent others, they'd most likely die and become zombies, exacerbating the problem. I knew the score about the creatures and I'd already figured out a little about hunting them from that first op." He shrugged as if it was no big deal. "I knew I could do this without risking too much and save other guys' lives in the bargain. What choice did I have?"

It went without saying that he could have chosen to stay out of it. He wasn't in the military anymore. He didn't have to follow orders unless he chose to.

"So you were going to retire even before you got bitten?"

He nodded. "It was all arranged. A job was all lined up for me with the mercs. That came in handy when Sykes wanted to hire me. Everything's being run through the merc company in the swamp. In reality, I'm an independent contractor for both the merc group and Sykes. Having the mercs as middle man helps keep the paperwork muddled enough so nobody will ever figure out what exactly Uncle Sam hired me to do or where I'm doing it."

"Convenient." She finished her sandwich and reached for her glass of milk, finishing that, too. There was a holder with paper napkins on the table and she took one to rid herself of crumbs.

"That's a specialty of theirs. When a job is too distasteful to run through official channels, the independent contractors ride to the rescue. Or so their recruiters say. Personally, I wasn't convinced until it happened to me."

"Do you plan to stay with the mercenary group after this mission is over?" She tried not to show how much that worried her.

"Frankly, with what they're paying me, I could retire tomorrow and be well off for the rest of my life. It pays well to be the only person in the world who can safely hunt zombies." He winked at her comically and even through her exhaustion, she had to laugh. "Honestly, I don't know. I'll no doubt take some time off. Preferably on some tropical island with an umbrella drink in my hand and warm waves lapping at my toes." He ate silently for a moment, polishing off the last of the sandwiches. "What about you, Mari? You're retiring in a few weeks. What plans have you made? Nobody on base seems to know where you'll go next."

"You've been asking around about me?" She was just sleepy enough to tease him with more candor than she would've otherwise used.

"A good soldier always does detailed recon." His smug expression prompted her to throw her balled-up napkin at him. He ducked with a grin. "So what are your plans? Got a job waiting?"

She pretended to fume for a moment more before relenting. "Actually, I was going to take some time off myself. I've had a few offers, from private practice to a big city hospital, but I haven't made up my mind yet. I thought I deserved a long vacation before I jump back in with both feet. In fact, your tropical paradise sounds like just the ticket."

"Great minds think alike." He saluted her with his glass and drained it. "Now what are your feelings about bed? I need to crash and all I can think about is your nice soft sheets, that comfortable mattress, and you tucked close in my arms. My own personal hot water bottle."

If she'd had another napkin in her hand, she would've

thrown that, too, as he got up and put their dishes in the sink. She loved his teasing. When he teased, he was truly comfortable. It was when he was tense that he became the serious soldier she had known for the first few weeks of their courtship. When he relaxed was when he was at his most charming, and most desirable. At least to her.

"I don't like being called a hot water bottle, Simon. That's not exactly a compliment." She pretended to be annoyed by his unflattering comparison.

"To me it is." He grabbed her around the waist as she stood, drawing her back against his chest, nuzzling her neck playfully. "I dream about hot water bottles when I'm stuck on the cold ground in a bivouac. I've even fantasized about hot water bottles a time or two when I was doing cold weather training in Alaska. Mariana-shaped hot water bottles, who called my name as I made them come."

"You have a very kinky imagination." Mock outrage filled her breathless words as he cupped her breasts through the thin fabric of her T-shirt.

"You love my kinky imagination, Mari. Come on, admit it." He nipped her earlobe and she squirmed in his arms. Damn, the man still knew just how to touch her to make her burn.

"I plead the Fifth." She reached back to tangle her hands in the short hairs at the back of his neck, pushing her breasts more fully into his grasp. His hands went up under her T-shirt and right to the front clasp of her bra, parting it so he could touch her skin. Mariana whimpered and moaned.

"Then admit this, Mari. Admit you want me." He whispered in her ear, his warm breath sliding past her defenses to fan the flame of arousal in her blood.

"Yes, Simon. I want you. I always want you."

His low chuckle made her squirm. "Now that's the kind of thing I like to hear."

He turned with her in his arms and walked them both out of the kitchen toward the bedroom. Her shirt was tossed off along the way, as was her bra. Her jeans ended up in a heap next to his at the door to her bedroom.

She pushed at his shirt until he, too, was naked and they tumbled onto the bed together. Their limbs tangled and twined as he sought and captured her mouth with his. The kiss was tempestuous, like nothing that had come before. They rolled until she was on top, her thighs spread on either side of his hips, ready in an instant to take him and ride him to oblivion. Simon had always been able to flip her switch with a single touch. Mariana slowed down, a moment of sanity prevailing. Protection first.

Reaching for her nightstand drawer, she fished out a condom from her dwindling emergency supply and ripped the package open. Sliding down his thighs, she took her time about covering him, enjoying the way he watched her, his eyes half lidded and oh so sexy.

"Don't tease, Mari. Come back up here."

"In good time." She leaned in closer to use her tongue on his exposed skin. She liked the way he twitched in her hands.

"No time like the present." His words were strained and his fists were clenched at his sides. Oh yeah, she was getting to him.

A grin spread across her face as she prowled up his body, trailing her lips and tongue over his abdomen and chest. He was hot, hard, and ridged in all the right places and she relished the opportunity to discover him all over again. It had been months since they'd been together and the previous day had been a blur of urgent need. There hadn't really been a chance for her to study him in detail.

"You've aged well, Simon. I think you're even more muscular than you were before. Have you been working out?"

The half-teasing question startled a laugh out of him. He reached for her, sliding his hands under her arms and lifting her over him. Yes, indeed, he must have been working out. At least, he was a lot stronger than she remembered.

"I've lived in interesting times since I last saw you, Mari." His expression clouded just for a second and she realized there was more truth to his words than he wanted to let on. "It makes a man hard." He realized his double entendre and gave her a lopsided grin. "Scratch that. *You* make me hard. You always have, sweetheart. Now what are you going to do about it?"

She straddled him, sliding over his hardness with teasing intensity. His eyes followed her movements, half lidded and sexy.

"I believe you deserve a reward for all that hard living." She teased as she took the tip of him inside. Little by little, she lowered over him, enjoying the feel of him stretching her. She was still just a little sore from the marathon they'd engaged in the day before but she went at a slow pace, allowing her body time to adjust.

"I like your rewards, ma'am." Simon lifted his hips gently, joining them fully.

"If you're good, I may have to reward you again, soldier." She gasped as she settled over him, taking him fully. She loved the way he felt inside her. For just a moment, she held position, cataloging the feel of him, the width and breadth of him, the way they fit so perfectly together. Nothing and no one had ever felt as right as Simon did.

"Oh, I plan to be very, very good." His teasing tone made her laugh and the moment was lost. She had to move. It was a biological and spiritual imperative.

Mariana repositioned herself, arranging her legs to give her better purchase, then began a slow, sliding rhythm. She shimmied her hips to get his full attention and his sleepy gaze rose from watching the place where they joined, pausing at her bouncing breasts momentarily and then finally to meet her gaze. She licked her lips, offering him a sinful smile.

"Like what you see?" Her head tilted to one side playfully.

"More than like, as I'm sure you can tell." He winked at her and moved his hands to her hips, guiding her into a faster rhythm. "Lean down here and I'll show you how much."

She did as he asked and his hands rose to cup her breasts. He knew just how to touch her to make her whimper with need. Just how much pressure to use to draw out her most explosive response.

"That much, eh?" She leaned into him, trying for a sexy grin. She must've succeeded because his fingers contracted, just slightly, and she saw his eyes darken with even deeper desire.

"Play time's over." In a split second, he moved his hands to her back, supporting her as he rolled them over so that she was flat on her back on the bed and he rose over her. "Now let me show you just how good I can be." He nipped her neck before drawing back, kneeling between her spread thighs as he began a rough, urgent pace that grew in intensity with each long stroke.

All coherent thought fled as he possessed her, pushed her higher, lost all control in the glorious union of their bodies. She surrendered all to him and felt his surrender in return. At least, that's what it felt like. That's what she thought she read in his eyes. What she felt in every touch of his body, every stroke that claimed her, pleasured her and turned her inside out.

"Come for me now, Mari. Come with me." His deep voice spurred her on, ordering her desire, commanding her pleasure. She could do nothing but comply, her body responding to his mastery as she had never responded to any other man.

Mariana shuddered as he pounded into her in short digs. Her climax hit her all at once, rocketing her to the sky and back down, only to climb even higher on the next wave. She screamed his name as he groaned. She felt him surge into her one last time as they both came hard. Together.

Dare she hope it could last forever?

CHAPTER 8

Simon realized he must've slept far longer than he had intended. The sun was low in the sky, but there was still time to eat and make love to his woman once more before he had to go out and hunt.

His woman. Man, that sounded right, though it was a problem all the way around. He hadn't intended to get mixed up with Mari again. He knew he'd hurt her the last time. In fact, it was kind of amazing she had forgiven him so easily. Regardless of her reasons, he was thankful for the past two days spent with her. It was a glimpse of Eden. Of what could have been if circumstances were different.

Mariana was such a special woman. If he had the luxury of planning for a lifetime, he would want to spend it with someone just like her. Who was he fooling? He wanted to spend it with *her*. No one else. Only Mariana.

She was the perfect woman for him. She matched him in every way. In fact, she far outclassed him in many ways. If she could put up with some of his more barbaric inclinations—which she had already demonstrated she could—then as a life partner, she would be perfect.

Too bad his life was totally fucked up at present. The zombie attack had changed him in fundamental ways. He didn't know how long the changes would last or if at some point in the future, they'd become fatal to him. He shouldn't be thinking about the lonely decades possibly to come. He shouldn't be dreaming about a life with Mariana in it. Not even a little.

But he couldn't help himself. Just like he couldn't help touching her, wanting her, making love to her. When she was near, all his best intentions went right out the window. And when she was in danger, all his protective instincts went on high alert. Nothing would happen to her on his watch. Nothing.

What happened after this crisis was over, well, that was up in the air. Right now, he would enjoy the days in her company and keep watch by night. He'd left her once and it had almost destroyed him. Only the thought that he'd done it for her own good had allowed him to stay away after his miraculous recovery from the zombie bite.

He didn't even have a scar to show for that horrific attack. In fact, he hadn't scarred since, and the scars he'd already carried on his body from his life before, faded more with each passing day. He'd become like something out of a comic book and the only doctor he trusted, aside from Mariana, didn't know how long the effect would last, or even if it wouldn't somehow turn dangerous later.

There were too many questions surrounding his condition. Too many variables in his life. Too much danger to drag Mariana into it again. No matter how badly he wanted her there, next to him, in his home and in his bed. For as long as he lived. However long that might be.

"What time is it?" Mariana's voice greeted him from the other side of her bed.

"About six, I think." He pulled her into his arms, spooning her from behind and gave her a smacking kiss on the temple. "You can sleep in, if you want."

She turned in his embrace, nibbling her way down his jaw to a particularly sensitive spot on his neck. "What if I don't want to sleep?"

"Well then, my mother taught me never to argue with a lady." He let his hands roam, cupping her softness and exploring the wet heat between her legs.

"What if I'm not a lady?" One of his hands tightened on her breast, rubbing the nipple between thumb and forefinger until she squirmed in pleasure.

"You're always a lady, Mari, even when you're a siren, luring men to your bed." He dipped his head and licked her nipple, soothing her and driving her higher. Sucking her in deep, he didn't let up until he heard her moan.

"Men?" Her voice was a breathy, teasing taunt. "There's only one man I'm interested in."

"Good thing." He lifted his head and turned her so she lay on her stomach. He then raised her hips and stuffed a pillow beneath to support her. Leaning close, he whispered in her ear. "Because I don't share." Finishing his possessive statement with a playful nip to her earlobe, he drew back, hovering over her, admiring the line of her sinuous back. Her skin glowed, enticing him. She truly was the siren he'd named her.

"Is that a promise?" She grinned at him over her shoulder, ever the coquette, and he felt his body tighten even more. She knew just what to say, just what to do, to make him want to explode.

The thing was, if he had his way, she would never know another man's touch again. He would never share her. He would keep her all to himself. But that was a dream for another time.

One hand drifted down her spine to her core, testing her readiness. She was warm, wet, and if her wiggling was any indication, more than willing.

Reaching into the open drawer in her nightstand, he fished out another condom and made short work of slipping it on. Then he bent over her, surrounding her with his larger frame to whisper in her ear.

"Do you want me, Mari?"

"Yes." Her breath caught as he moved into position

behind her. He liked that. Oh, yes, he liked that very much, indeed.

"How much?" He teased her wet folds with the tip of his cock. She was quivering, just slightly, around him.

"Simon! I want you more than anything. Please. Oh, please." She gasped as he slid into her from behind. She was morning soft and wet with arousal, making his way easy.

"That's my girl." He tried to keep his rhythm slow and easy but she was too much for him. She always had been. No other woman could make him so hot so fast or keep him on the knife's edge longer. Only his Mari.

He stroked into her deep, hard, and long, just the way he knew she liked it. He guided her hips as she began to move back against him, urging him onward, into an ever increasing rhythm.

"Faster, Simon!" Her voice became hoarse with reaction as her head thrashed.

"Your wish," he panted as he sped his thrusts, "is my command."

Before long, she was making those little sounds of arousal on every inward glide and he felt her inner muscles clench around him. The grip of her body gave him that little extra edge of sensation that only she had ever given him.

"Are you with me, baby?" His hands cupped her hips, gripping hard as he pressed within her.

"Simon." His name was drawn from her lips as two separate, long syllables. Yeah, his little tigress was with him. "Simon! I'm so close."

So was he. It wouldn't take much more. All he wanted was for her to come hard, and she would take him with her. Reaching under her with one hand, he teased her clit with his fingers. She clenched hotly around him and screamed his name. Music to his ears.

Oh yeah. She was coming and he wasn't far behind.

"Do it, baby. Do it for me."

She cried out and her body shook beautifully around him. A second later, he followed her over, into the void where only pleasure existed. The two of them and the greatest pleasure he'd ever known, or would ever know. The pleasure of Mari. His Mari. His woman.

It took a long time for them to recover. Eventually the glow of the setting sun, just visible around the edges of Mariana's bedroom curtains, roused them both to action. Simon got up and grabbed a five-minute shower, then left the bathroom to Mariana while he put together a simple meal in her kitchen for them to share.

"Mmm, what did you cook? It smells good." Mariana took him by storm, coming up behind him and enveloping him in that wonderful scent that was hers alone. He turned and took her into his arms for a lazy kiss. She was warm and her hair was still a bit damp from her shower. She felt like heaven to him.

"I raided your cupboards. Hope you don't mind."

"I don't mind a bit. What's mine is yours."

Including her heart? He wasn't sure he really wanted to know. One part of him wanted her love, another part—the more sensible part—knew no good could come of it. He'd hurt her before and would likely hurt her again. He hoped, for her sake, she hadn't fallen in love with him. It was bad enough to leave her hurt. He would hate to leave her heartbroken as well.

"Let's eat, then I have to get out there. I want you safely locked in before dark."

They ate, making easy conversation. She told him about her life since they'd parted and amused him with funny stories from the research project she had been involved with until a few months ago.

"So you continued in research? I knew that's what you'd hoped to do."

"It took some time, but eventually a space opened up for me on a more advanced project. I was working on a live trial of dietary supplements, charting how different natural substances like vitamins and certain enzymes affected the performance of soldiers in the field. It was interesting work and the leader of the project, Doctor Amelia Jones, is a brilliant scientist. She promised to give me a sterling recommendation should I decide to try for a research post in civilian life. She doesn't do that often, so I guess I impressed her. She has a bit of a hardnosed reputation, but she's a truly gifted scientist. That grants her a lot of leeway."

"I have no doubt you wowed her with your brilliance." He meant every word. Mariana possessed one of the brightest minds he had ever encountered. "So how did you end up manning the clinic?"

"Since I'm leaving the Navy shortly, they wanted to give me time to train my replacement on the research team. They managed to get him early, so I wound up with a little overlapping time. The clinic needed staffing after the last rotation. I've been here for a few months working out the rest of my time. Lucky for you."

"Very lucky for me, indeed." He toasted her with his water glass as they finished their meal of canned soup, vegetables, and salad from Mariana's refrigerator.

Simon would have said more, but just then his phone came to life, vibrating urgently in his pocket.

He stood and moved into the living room for a few minutes to take the call. When he returned, he had his pack over his shoulder and was fishing out a clip of darts. He handed it to Mariana with a grim twist to his lips.

"Sykes was doing a flyover and spotted the mailman walking out in the open on Webster Road. He didn't look good." His expression darkened. "I'm going over there. You stay here and hunker down. I'll be back to check on you after I take care of this, before I go out again. That Marine is still out there and he gets cleverer by the day."

He drew her in for a quick hug and she kissed him with all the emotion she couldn't put into words. "Be careful, Simon."

"Always. You know how to reload the pistol, right?" He

pressed the clip of darts into her hand as she nodded. "I'll be back as soon as I can. Lock the door after me and stay out of sight."

He paused for one last kiss at the door and then he was gone, melting into the woods in the direction of Webster Road. He could've taken her SUV, but she knew Simon could get there in half the time by cutting through the woods, rather than taking the meandering backcountry roads.

Mariana reloaded the pistol first thing. She would have the full six shots if anything tried to get in. She had already barricaded the largest of the windows and locked the dead bolts on both doors. She decided to close off the bedroom and spare room and spend her time in the kitchen and living room. Those were the largest rooms in the house and both had doors to the outside. If anything sent her into retreat, she could always get out of the house and make a run for it, barring unforeseen circumstances.

About fifteen minutes after Simon left, she heard a noise outside, on the far side of the house. Tiptoeing into the spare room she took a look out the window. That room had a good vantage point for that side of the house.

Her skittering pulse pounded in her ears when she saw the shape of a man walking steadily toward the house from the woods. His face was intact, but his skin looked a ghastly gray and his eyes were menacingly vacant. He was wearing blood spattered fatigues. This was the last missing Marine and he was heading straight for her house.

Mariana dialed Simon's number and prayed while the phone rang. He picked up on the second ring.

"Simon, he's here! The Marine. He just walked out of the woods and he's heading for the house."

"Hold tight, Mari. I'm on my way. The mailman was a diversion. I got him, but he led me on quite a chase. I'm out past Webster Road and will have to double back. Stay hidden if you can."

She heard a scratching sound against the side of the house and saw the Marine round the corner. He was heading for the front.

"He's going around front," she whispered, desperate fear edging into her voice.

"Stay out of sight, Mari." It sounded like he was running and his voice was breathy.

She headed for the front of the house, wanting to keep tabs on where the zombie was, so she could avoid him. She heard a bang and her heart leapt into her throat.

As she entered the living room, the small window nearest her smashed and a fist opened just feet from her head. Long, yellow claws tipped the fingers on a hand that had once been human. She still didn't really understand what it was about the contagion that made their nails grow to hard claws after death, but thought it was probably as part of the semi-petrifaction process. The thought came out of the part of her mind that could still reason, the part that observed the unfolding events in a sort of calm horror.

The rest of her was scared shitless and trembling in fear.

She screamed as the clawed hand rent the air in front of her face.

"What's going on?" Simon demanded, his voice a tinny shout from the tiny speaker in the phone.

"He broke through the window in the living room, but it's too small. He can't get in that way."

Apparently the zombie realized that at around the same time. The arm retreated from the broken window and the creature moved to the front door. Running, Mariana threw whatever furniture she could in front of it, barring the way. The couch, the small bookcase, a chair, and whatever else she could scrounge went in front of the solid wooden door.

Just in time, as it turned out. The creature began pounding against the door. It sounded like he was throwing all his weight against it and she watched in terror as the pile of furniture began to move—just slightly—inward.

"Hold on, Mari. I'm—"

The call disconnected. She'd lost contact with Simon!

The phone was dead in her hand and she didn't dare spare

the time to redial. She had to take care of herself until he could get here. She had the pistol and if she could get a clear shot, she'd take it.

Maneuvering around to the side, she watched the gap between the broken door and the pile of furniture widen by slow degrees. When the arm reached through again she aimed and fired. She tried to hit the fleshy part of his upper arm, but missed. This one was faster than the others she'd seen. He'd pulled his arm back hastily when the pistol went off, ruining her shot.

She still had five darts loaded and a few more in the kitchen if it came to that. The eerie sort of moaning sound the others had made transformed into loud groaning and grunting sounds with this one. He was stronger, too. He looked as if he had been in the prime of life when he'd died, at the peak of his physical strength and stamina.

Mariana was in trouble. This one wouldn't go down as easy as Becky Sue. He was no soft civilian. This was a highly trained soldier. She wasn't sure if it made any difference, but this guy had to be one of the first zombies created in the lab. His face was still intact from what she'd seen, though oddly discolored, as was the rest of his skin.

He was probably responsible for making others like him—for killing innocent civilians, including Becky Sue, her grandmother, and the poor postman. This was a killing machine spawning horror in its wake.

He shouldered through the widening opening in the door and she fired again.

"Shit!" She missed again as he jerked back. She was down to four rounds in her pistol. She had to make them count.

The pile of furniture moved again; the gap between door and barricade widened an inch more. Mariana eyed the furniture pile. In another two or three inches, the couch would wedge up against where the closet wall jutted out from the far wall. It would be nearly impossible to move after that unless something in the pile of furniture shifted or broke under the creature's weight.

But he would also be a few more inches into the house. Would that be enough for him to squeeze inside? She said a quick prayer that it wouldn't.

Just in case, she backed toward the kitchen door. She could barricade herself in there if she had to and still be able to flee through the back door if he managed to get into the living room and made inroads on the door leading from there into the kitchen. It was a sound plan. Too bad she was shaking like a leaf contemplating her retreat.

She just had to buy time until Simon could get here. He had been after this creature for weeks now. He would put an end to this thing once and for all, as was only fitting.

Unless she got a clear shot in the meantime, of course. The zombie shouldered farther into her living room and she took another shot. Another miss. She cursed herself. She was better than this but panic was making her take chances she shouldn't be taking.

Three darts left in the pistol. The couch bumped up against the closet wall and stuck. Ominous snapping sounds told her some of the furniture pile wasn't holding up and the barricade moved a lot farther inward than she expected. Time to retreat.

Mariana saw the creature. He actually made eye contact. His eyes were narrowed as if in anger, but otherwise blank. He saw her, but there wasn't any real sign of life in his gaze, only a vapid intentness that sent chills down her spine.

She fired one last shot and retreated through the kitchen door. He flinched, but she couldn't be sure if it was from being hit by her dart, or a quick move that saved him from it. Either way, he was too close. She had to retreat.

She scrambled into the kitchen and moved the refrigerator, table, chairs, and anything else she could in front of the door that led from the living room to the kitchen. The zombie might get into the living room. She had conceded that ground. If he tried to get in here, though, she would be able to retreat through the door leading to her backyard. It was locked, of course, but she could flip the dead bolt and be through it in a matter of seconds, if necessary.

Increasingly loud noises from the other room told her he had gained entrance to the living room. Loud crashes made her cringe and shiver in fear as she heard things being thrown around and breaking. Then it got quiet. These creatures didn't make a whole lot of sound unless they were pounding on something or making those pathetic moaning sounds that were almost sub-vocal. You had to be close to hear them.

"Come on, Simon," she whispered, urging him to get here soon.

She needed help. She wasn't afraid to admit it. She was a doctor, not a highly trained special ops warrior used to dealing with the worst of the worst although she had been getting plenty of real world experience the last few days. More than she had ever expected and certainly more than she'd ever wanted. She would gladly trade in all this excitement for a nice, normal, hectic day treating patients. She wouldn't have wanted to give up her time with Simon, but she would happily trade in the zombies for a bunch of unruly patients any day.

The sounds from the other room died down, and she tiptoed toward the back door to see if she could find out what was going on. Where the heck was Simon?

Mariana approached the window in the back door from an oblique angle, just in case, but she couldn't see much. Little by little, she edged more fully toward the small window. Everything looked clear, so she faced the small pane fully—and came face to face with the zombie.

She screamed and lunged away from the window, back toward the countertop where she had left the extra darts. She still had two in her pistol and she intended to make them count.

Her close-up look at the Marine's face gave her details she wished she hadn't seen. His flesh was gray. The area all around his mouth and between his yellowed teeth was stained brown with dried blood. Simon had told her they liked to bite and undoubtedly this one had done his share of chewing on his victims.

The man reared back and then his fist punched inward, breaking through the thick security glass of the little window as if it were nothing. When she saw him reaching inward, looking for the doorknob, she knew she was in serious trouble. This one was way smarter than the others.

His fingers found the knob for the dead bolt and turned it. Then he reached farther down toward the small dimpled lever on the doorknob itself. If he turned that, the door would be fully unlocked and all he would have to do then...

Mariana steadied her shaking arm as best she could and took careful aim. Firing, she hit the thing's arm, up near the biceps. The dart stuck and held, but the creature didn't slow. He turned the final lock and then the doorknob, dragging his arm out of the small window, dislodging the dart as he pulled it through the tight space.

She watched the dart clatter to the floor with a sinking heart. Had he gotten enough of the toxin? Had the dart been stuck in him long enough to deliver its full dose? How long before the toxin took full effect? Would she have enough time before he cornered her?

Her thoughts raced as she backed as far away as she could. She pulled the kitchen table and chairs off the pile barricading the inner door and threw them between herself and the zombie at the back door. She could never get everything moved out of the way in time, but she preferred to die fighting if she had to, not fleeing, her back to the danger. No, she would face it head on.

She only wished Simon knew what he truly meant to her. She wished she had told him how much she loved him. How much she always had...and always would.

Regrets. She had so many where he was concerned. Through the fear that rode her, she knew her regrets were best saved for another time. Now was the time for action. Her fate would be decided in the next few minutes.

The door opened, slamming back against its frame as the Marine pushed inside. He moved faster than the other zombies she'd seen, but she wouldn't give up without a fight. Mariana squeezed off her remaining round, lodging it squarely in his chest.

She knew the toxin took time to work. Would she make it? Did she have enough time? She pulled out two darts from the spares—one for each hand. She would stab the son of a bitch with them if he got too close. She would go down fighting if it was the last thing she did.

He stalked closer, moving quickly now, picking up her kitchen chairs and throwing them aside. Only the table stood between her and the zombie.

And then he began to dissolve.

His legs fell out from under him, stopping his forward motion, then his torso disintegrated, falling to the floor in a shower of organic matter. Then she saw the large darts from Simon's rifle.

He had to have shot the zombie in the back while it was still out in the yard. His rifle had a much longer range than her small pistol. He'd taken the shots from far out, maybe while running to her rescue. Her darts hadn't had enough time to work. Simon's darts had been there first, in the creature's back, doing their job in the nick of time. Thank heaven.

A second later, Simon burst through her back door. She was never more grateful to see him. He'd saved her life.

"Mari? Did he touch you?"

"No, Simon. Oh, God, it's so good to see you."

She flew into his arms, climbing over the table and jumping the pile of debris that had been the zombie. She almost knocked Simon backward, but he steadied her, his powerful arms coming around her and holding her tight while he rained kisses down over her face.

"God, baby, I thought I'd lost you. I can't, Mari. I can't ever lose you." His whispered words were music to her ears.

"I love you, Simon. I wanted you to know. My one regret when I thought I was going to die was that I'd never told you. I've loved you for a long time. Since we were first dating. And

I never stopped loving you, even when you left."

"Oh, Mari. I need you so much." He kissed her then, a long, lingering kiss. Mariana was beside herself with relief and joy. She had finally admitted the love that had never waned in her heart for him.

She wrapped herself around him in both delight and relief. He'd saved her life, no doubt about that. There hadn't been enough time for her darts to do the job. Simon's longer-range rifle darts had saved her.

Now that the danger was past, she was free to let her emotions take over. Tears mixed with the joy in her heart, sliding down her face and into their kiss. Simon pulled back, concern in his gaze. His expression was completely open to her for the first time and she could see the love shining in his eyes, the care in every beloved line of his face.

"You're all right, Mari. You're safe."

"I know. I'm just feeling a little overwhelmed. That's the last one, right? You're through with hunting them?"

"As far as I know, he was the last and the most difficult to catch. He's been evading me for months."

"He seemed smarter than the others."

"He was. He set the mailman up as a distraction, near as I can tell. He waited for me to go after that poor soul before attacking you here. None of the others showed that much initiative or cognitive ability."

"I'll freely admit, he scared the shit out of me. I don't ever want to go through anything even remotely like that again."

He hugged her close, stroking her back. "It's over, Mari. I think that's the last of them, but I'll probably be prowling around for the next few nights, just to make sure."

"And where will you be spending your days?" She challenged him, daring to hope his declaration meant he would be willing to stay with her this time, to see where their relationship might lead.

"I'll spend my days making love with you, if you're available." He winked at her, a devilish grin on his face.

"I'll see what I can arrange," she teased back. "I do have a bit of leave left that I really should use up."

"I'd be honored to help you find something to do with all your free time, Doctor." He lowered his head again and kissed her deeply, but all too briefly. He straightened. "Hold that thought. I need to report this to Sykes so he can get containment on Webster Road before any civilians go through there. Then I'm taking you to the nearest hotel so they can scrub this place and put it back to rights. Go pack a few things while I make the call."

She did as he asked, glad to have a task to occupy her hands and her mind. She was still dizzy from fright and from the amazing turn of events. Simon had saved her life and he'd admitted some pretty deep feelings for her. She didn't know which event was more amazing.

She had gone from stark terror to utter despair to grim resolution and then to blessed relief, all in the space of an hour or two. Her emotions were definitely on overload and spending what was left of the night at a hotel sounded like an awesome idea.

CHAPTER 9

"Let me get that for you." Simon made short work of moving the refrigerator and other pieces of her make-shift barricade out of the way so she could get into the rest of the house.

He preceded her into the living room, to assess the damage and make certain everything was truly safe. He hated seeing the devastation on her pretty face when she looked at the ruin of her living room.

"Oh, boy." She sighed sadly. "This place is a disaster."

The monster had trashed the living room. Many of her ornaments and knickknacks were broken, as was a lot of her furniture. Otherwise, it was safe enough. The zombie hadn't left any nasty surprises that he could find.

"Let's check out the rest of the house before I make my call."

"Thanks, Simon." She tugged on his sleeve, her little hand stealing into his for a quick squeeze.

He leaned down to place a quick, reassuring kiss on her lips. He wanted to make love to her, but safety, duty, and security had to come first. There would be plenty of time to get her mind off the horrific events of the night. The rest of their lives, if he had his way.

"Come on, sweetheart. The sooner we do this, the sooner we can get out of here."

She seemed to gather herself before turning to the small hallway that led to the rest of the house. She had locked her bedroom, bathroom, and the door to the spare room. All were still locked. The creature hadn't even ventured down the hall from what Simon could see.

She unlocked all three doors one at a time at his signal and he checked each of the rooms out before he would let her enter. They were untouched, thankfully, and he watched as she grabbed a satchel and began tossing things in. He grabbed his bag, which he had left by the door to her bedroom, and went into the living room to make his call. Despite the late hour, Matt Sykes picked up on the first ring.

"It's done. We just got the last one at Mari's house. It was close. Bastard came right for her. That's the third time she's been in the line of fire with these things, Matt."

"She okay?" Sykes asked. Simon heard the concern in his buddy's voice. Matt Sykes was a good guy who truly cared about the people under his command, even if he seemed tough as nails on the outside.

"She's shaken, but she's a trooper. I want to get her out of here though. The guy trashed her living room and cornered her in the kitchen. What's left of him is in there. I'll tag it on the way out. There's also another down on Webster Road. The mailman. The one that attacked Mari set the mailman up as a distraction."

Matt Sykes whistled on the other end of the line. "I didn't think they were capable of that kind of forethought and planning."

"Neither did I. This last one's been a thorn in my side for weeks. He was a lot cannier than the others."

"You got him. That's all that matters. Good work, Si. By the numbers, that should be the end of it, but I want you to stay in position for another week or two, just to be sure."

"Roger that. But I'm done for tonight. I'm taking Mari to a hotel. She's been through a lot."

"Good idea. Put it on the tab. We'll spring for the accommodations while we put her house to rights. The containment team will be there shortly. When they're done I'll send a carpenter out to fix her place up good as new."

"Thanks, Matt. I'll let her know. I'm sure she'll appreciate it."

They spoke a few more minutes about the mission and what came next. By the time they ended the call, Mari was ready. She stood in the hall, waiting for him, the packed satchel in her hands. He took the bag from her and slung it over his shoulder along with his own.

They had to go out through the kitchen because the front door was still mostly blocked. Simon dropped a small transmitter on the debris that had once been a Marine. He had been a hell of an adversary but all in all, it was better that he was now gone. Simon pitied the man who had come to such an untimely and unnatural fate.

The sky was turning gray in the east as they walked together around the house, a sure sign of the dawn to come.

"Give me your keys, sweetheart. I'll drive."

She didn't argue, just handed the keys over. Her hands were trembling, and he knew she was still dealing with the residue of the adrenaline surges that had helped save her life.

He opened her door, checked the interior of the SUV, and ushered her in. Stowing his gear and the two packs in back, he then claimed the driver's seat. They rode in silence for a while as Simon negotiated the gravel lane that led to the larger paved road. He hadn't driven in this area much, but he knew the layout from both map study and reconnaissance. He knew just where to head to find the nicest hotel in town.

"I'm glad that's over." Mariana shut her eyes as she collapsed back against the headrest.

"Me, too." He reached over and took her hand.

"You're out of a job now." Her attempt at humor warmed him.

"Can't say I'm sorry about it." He took the turn toward the highway. There were a series of hotels out toward the city at a variety of price points. The one he had in mind was top of the line and luxurious. Mari deserved a little pampering after what she had experienced over the past few days.

She dozed on the way and Simon understood the adrenaline that had been keeping her going had also caused her to bottom out. Her body was crashing after the hell she had been through that night. He pulled in to the circular drive of the upscale hotel and despite the hour, a bellman and a valet were ready for them.

Simon touched her cheek. "Wake up, love. We're here. Just a few more minutes and you can go to sleep in a big, comfy, king-size bed. What do you say?"

"Is that a promise?" She didn't even open her eyes and her voice was sleepy.

"Scout's honor."

She propped one eyelid open. "Were you ever a scout?"

"Not a boy scout. But I took scout training. I'm the real deal," he teased.

"I have no doubt about that, Simon." She straightened, stretching as she came more fully awake. Her expression was serious when she turned to him in the dim interior of the car. "If I never said it before, I've always admired your skills in the field, even if I never really experienced them until the past few days. You saved my life more than once and I'll always be grateful."

"I don't want your gratitude, Mari." The conversation turned serious real fast.

"It's way more than gratitude, Simon." Her eyes met his and the moment stretched.

She had said she loved him. He hugged those words close to his battered heart. He wanted to reach out and grab onto her with both hands and just hold her for the rest of their lives. But how could he take a chance with her future? How could he not? Simon moved closer, on the verge of declaring himself.

There was a noise by the driver's side door.

He mentally cursed the valet who chose that moment to

walk up to his window. Her gaze flickered to the intrusive presence at the window, and the mood was broken.

Simon wasn't sure if he was more annoyed or grateful. In that moment he'd been tempted to throw all caution to the wind. Now, saner thoughts prevailed. Any more insanity on his part would have to wait until they were inside.

"Come on, let's get checked in."

He hopped out of the SUV and dealt with the valet while she exited the car and stretched some more. She was about to get their bags when he stopped her, utilizing the bellman's services. This sojourn was all about pampering her. Starting right now, he wouldn't let her lift a finger.

He checked them in using the company credit account, and within minutes they were ensconced in a luxury suite with a lovely view of the city far below. She hadn't said much on the way up in the elevator and was yawning a lot. The poor woman was beat. Simon's first priority had to be her comfort—getting her settled in a warm bed with nothing to do but sleep until she woke naturally.

Simon was used to the letdown after an extreme adrenaline rush and was better able to deal with it. Poor Mari was trying hard to keep her eyes open, but was losing the battle when he ushered the bellman out with a hefty tip.

"Alone at last." He leaned back against the closed door and couldn't help the grin that spread across his face. She was tousled and adorably sleepy, perched on the foot of the king-size bed.

"I'm sorry, Simon. I seem to be dead on my feet." She made a face. "Sorry. Bad choice of words there."

He laughed in spite of himself. It was a good sign that she was already able to joke about what they'd just been through.

"How about you just relax and I'll take care of you for a change?" He pushed away from the door and walked toward her.

"That sounds interesting." She perked up a little.

"Do you feel up to a hot bath? There's a Jacuzzi in there." He jerked his chin toward the door to the spacious bathroom.

"There's also a bottle of wine in the cooler. After a glass or two, you should be mellow enough to sleep straight through."

"After a glass of wine and a hot bath I'll be comatose, Simon." She laughed and the sound warmed his heart.

"That's okay. Your only job now is to sleep until you can sleep no more."

"What about the clinic? I have to go back on duty tomorrow—or rather, today. What time is it?" She searched for the clock on the nightstand next to the big bed.

"Don't worry, it's all arranged. Commander Sykes is going to square things. You're off duty for the next three days at least. More if you need it. All we have to do is let him know."

"I'm impressed. It must be nice to have friends in high places." She gave him a teasing smile as he took her hand and helped her rise to her feet.

"You've earned a rest after what you've been through the past few days. Matt Sykes agreed. He also wanted me to thank you for pitching in on my mission." He walked her toward the bathroom door, ushering her through into the white wonderland of porcelain and steel.

"Oh, this looks like heaven." She ran her hand over the gleaming countertop as they passed on their way to the tub. Simon reached down to start the taps then returned to help her undress.

"My version of heaven is right here." He cupped her shoulders and looked down into her sleepy eyes. His words came out in a rough whisper, clogged with emotion. He knew he shouldn't speak of his feelings, but found he couldn't help himself.

"Do you really mean that, Simon?" She looked so hopeful as she stared up at him, searching his gaze.

"More than anything, Mari. You've always been it for me. Since the moment I first met you, I haven't wanted anyone but you in my life." She looked responsive so he dared a little more. "For always."

"Always?" Her whisper sounded full of anxious hope, sparking the same feeling in him.

He nodded. "I know I don't have any right to ask…" He trailed off, uncertain, then started again. "I want to be with you, Mari. I want to try again, and I promise I won't leave this time. You'll have to kick me out of your life if you want me gone, because I don't think I can give you up. It nearly killed me the first time and I'm not strong enough to put myself through that again. Even though I'm asking you to deal with the uncertainty I'm facing. I mean, they don't really know what the contagion did to me. I could have complications later—"

She stilled his tumbling words by placing one of her fingers over his lips, but the beatific smile on her lovely face reassured him.

"I want you in my life, too, Simon." Her voice was laced with tears. They looked like happy tears, judging by the delicate smile on her face. "Your condition doesn't bother me. I'll take you any way I can get you. Remember, I'm a doctor, and not a bad researcher. If you're willing, I'd be happy to see what I can discover about what happened to you and what could happen in the future. I want to help in any way I can, Simon. You mean a lot to me."

"You mean a lot to me, too, Mari."

It wasn't a declaration of love but it would do for now, Simon thought. He had to work his way up to saying the words. He wanted to hear her say them again first. He didn't want to be the only one out there on that most fragile of limbs. He had gone pretty far up the tree already. That final gamble would be better saved for another time when they were both rested and able to think more clearly.

The Jacuzzi really was heaven. Mariana felt boneless between the warm, gushing water and Simon's hands stroking over her. The tub was big enough for them both and Simon had brought in the wine and two glasses shortly after he'd helped her into the full tub. Then he'd undressed and climbed in behind her, spooning her from behind.

The combination of the wine, the warm water, and the hot

man behind her had her in a state of relaxation she hadn't felt in a long time. In fact, she didn't think she had ever felt so good. At least not in recent memory. Probably not since the last time she and Simon had been together.

"This is nice," she said, trailing her fingers through the water.

"More than nice," Simon agreed from behind her.

"Someday I'm going to get one of these tubs for my house."

"In that little cabin? I don't think it'd fit. You'd have to add on a room."

"No, the cabin is a rental. I mean, when I buy a house. I'll probably be moving out of the area once I'm out of the Navy, depending on what job I take next, and…where you'll be."

She felt his muscles tense behind her and waited with held breath for his response.

"Would you come live with me if I promised to put in a Jacuzzi?" The words were teasing, but she thought the sentiment was very real. It made her warm all over. He was asking her to live with him. Hopefully that was a first step toward a lifetime together and she would take it—she would take *him*—any way she could get him.

"With an enticement like that, how could I refuse?" She reached behind her, twisting to pull his head down for a tender kiss. The warm water and his strong arms combined to make her forget all her troubles, all the fear and worry that had gone before.

"I think you'll like my place in the country. How do you feel about chickens?"

"We had chickens when I was a kid. And a couple of geese. I could never eat the ones we raised and wouldn't let anybody near them if butchering had been mentioned. My family used to laugh at me, but those birds were like pets."

"Duly noted." He chuckled at her, as she'd known he would. "How about if we get a few hens for eggs and let them live out their lives on the farm? No hen stew."

"You'd do that for me?"

"For you, I'd move mountains."

He sounded so calm about them living together and she could picture his little farm in her mind. It was like a fairy tale. A dream come true. She hugged the image to her heart, daring to hope for the first time that it might really come to pass.

They languished in the tub for a few more minutes. She would have loved to make love to him, but she just didn't have the energy. The steam made her sleepy and the feeling of security and happiness that only Simon gave her lulled her into a dreamlike state.

She was half asleep when he coaxed her out of the bath, dried her off, and ushered her toward the bed. He had been so good to her. She'd been able to banish the horrors of the past few days almost completely from her mind while he pampered her. She would have loved to do the same for him but she was too tired, too drained after the trip here and the night they'd just passed. She would make it up to him later. When they woke up. For now, she reveled in the feel of him lying next to her as he tucked them both into the huge, fluffy bed. She hugged the thought of living with him close to her heart. It was a start. He wasn't pushing her out of his life. He wasn't pushing her away anymore. They'd live together, and wherever life took them, they'd face it as a team.

He spooned with her, tucking her close against his warm body, making her feel safe. For the first time in days, she felt truly safe. She could let down the guard she'd developed and let go, trusting to Simon to protect her. For always. That's what he'd said.

She hugged the memory of their conversation to her heart. Simon wasn't the most eloquent of men at the best of times, but he had come closer than he ever had to expressing some pretty powerful feelings. Feelings she returned fully.

"I love you, Simon," she whispered as she drifted to sleep in his arms.

CHAPTER 10

Mariana woke shivering in reaction to a nightmare she couldn't really remember. It wasn't hard to guess what she had been dreaming about. Her life for the past few days had been the stuff of horror movies.

"You okay?" Simon's gravelly voice came to her in the dim room. She turned to find him watching her, concern in his expression.

"Man, that was a doozy. Sorry I woke you." She wiped her face, not surprised to find tears on her cheeks. Her hand was shaking as faint tremors wracked her body. Adrenaline still coursed through her veins making her long to flee…somewhere. It made no sense, but nightmares never really did.

Simon tugged her into his arms, letting her nestle her head below his chin. One strong hand circled her waist while the other stroked gently over her hair in soothing motions. She felt cocooned in his warmth, in his protection.

"Listen to my heartbeat, Mari. Let it steady you. Breathe deep and let the adrenaline dissipate. You'll crash in a few minutes if you let go of the fear."

"Have some experience with this, do you?" She tried for calm despite the way her heart still raced. It was embarrassing to be so vulnerable, so afraid and trembling in his presence.

Simon was a modern-day warrior of iron will who didn't show fear. He probably didn't even feel it anymore. Not after all he'd been through. He had faced down zombies for the past few months as a matter of course. She felt like a fool for the unreasonable fear that had snuck up on her when she was most vulnerable. In her sleep. When all her defenses were down.

"I've learned to deal with the ups and downs of the adrenaline fog." Simon's husky voice touched her, drawing her away from the fright that still rode her body.

"You?" She moved back a few inches to look up at him. "I seriously doubt you ever feel fear."

"Oh, I feel it." His hand cupped her cheek, his thumb stroking her skin with a light touch. "Maybe not as easily as I used to after all I've seen, but believe me, it's there. I just don't show it like most people. I've learned to channel the adrenaline rush, to use it to make me stronger instead of giving me the shakes." His hand trailed down, over her shoulder to her arm, and then his fingers twined with hers, bringing their joined hands to his chest. "Your muscles still feel like overdone spaghetti?"

A laugh burst from her lips. "How'd you know?"

"I've been there." He flattened her hand on his chest, right over his heart. The rhythm was strong and steady, just like Simon himself. He was her rock in a sea of uncertainty. "Just concentrate on the rhythm of my heart, Mari. Breathe deep and slow. You'll get there in time."

She followed his instructions. Breathing in and out, focusing on his heartbeat, his comforting presence. After a few minutes, it started to work. She began to feel her heartbeat matching pace with his. Her breathing slowed and steadied as her body tuned itself to his.

"God, Simon, I feel like such a fool." Her voice still shook, but her breathing was leveling out, steadier now.

"Never that, sweetheart," he whispered, stroking her back. "You're the bravest, smartest, most beautiful woman I've ever known."

When he said it like that, she almost believed him. Simon had always had the ability to make her feel really good—emotionally and physically—with both his confidence in her, and his skills as a lover. Maybe a little of the latter was what she really needed to get her mind off the nightmare.

She rose above him on one elbow. "And you're the sexiest man I've ever had the good fortune to have in my bed." She gave him a temptress's smile. At least she hoped that's how he would interpret it. Beneath it all, she still felt a little desperate to forget all the scary things that had happened in the past few days.

"You think I'm sexy, eh?" His teasing grin told her he was willing to humor her whims. He knew her too well not to realize what she was doing, and he played along, the rogue.

"Oh, I know you're sexy. Sexy Simon. That's what my friend Claire used to call you behind your back. Do you remember her?" She trailed her fingers over his chest.

"Dark hair, kept in a bun all the time? Glasses? She was studying neurology, wasn't she?" She nodded, surprised he remembered such small details. That was a fair physical description of Claire, though she had a scintillating sense of humor under that sometimes severe exterior. They'd gone to happy hour a few times after work and on one or two memorable occasions, Simon and some of his friends had joined them at the local watering hole. "I didn't think she had it in her. Looked like an uptight librarian to me."

Mariana burst out laughing. "Yeah, I guess she does, but you know, librarians get a really bad rap. They're not all disapproving matron types. You'd like my sister, Ella. She's a librarian and she's nothing like the stereotype. She's boisterous and fun loving. She always has a smile and laughs easily. She was a real clown growing up."

"Sister, eh? Well, if she's your sister, I like her already."

She liked the way he teased her but she knew there was some kernel of truth in his words. He had always made an effort to be nice to her friends from work on the rare occasions they'd mingled. Like those happy hour gatherings. He had been polite and encouraging to Claire, who was surprisingly shy around Simon and his military buddies.

"I think she'll like you, too."

"You thinking about introducing me to your family? This sounds serious." His blue gaze glittered with an intense light and she was afraid maybe she'd assumed too much, too soon.

She forced herself to shrug noncommittally. "You'll meet them eventually, I'm sure. No doubt you'll be dragged to one of the family gatherings at some point. There are a few each year where we all get together on the farm, and pick on one another for old time's sake."

He took a minute before answering, which didn't do much to reassure her. "Sounds like fun."

It was time to change the subject. Lifting one knee, she straddled him, leaning forward over his muscular torso.

"So now that we're both awake, what do you think we should do to keep ourselves occupied?" She sent him a daring smile, hoping he'd take her up on her blatant offer. She had confidence he would, judging by his state of arousal. She could feel him stir against her bottom. Oh yeah, he'd play along.

"How about a little game?" The teasing tone of his voice warmed her once more.

"What kind of game?" She was willing to try just about anything with him and she had no doubt he knew it.

"What else? My favorite game. Simon Says."

"Oh, I like the way your mind works, sexy Simon."

One of his hands moved to her breast, cupping her with warmth and exploring fingers. "Sexy Simon then," he agreed. "Sexy Simon says to lean closer so I can kiss these nipples that both seem to want my attention." Their eyes met and fire leaped between them. "Do they, Mari? Do they want my attention?"

"Yes, Simon." Her voice was shaky already and he hadn't done much more than touch her.

"Well come on down here then, woman. Simon says."

She felt wanton as she leaned over him, following his orders. She had always enjoyed making love with him when he exercised his dominant streak, but this new, teasing, *sexy* Simon was something very exciting indeed.

He latched on to her nipple with his tongue, swirling it around the eager peak with just the right pressure. He used his teeth gently, never hurting, always enticing, and the suction of his mouth felt oh so good. Then he switched to the other side, letting his fingers take up where his mouth had left off, sliding in the wetness left by his lips to pinch and tease.

She moaned with pleasure and he drew back, releasing her nipple with a little pop.

"You like that?"

"You know I do." There was a breathless quality to her voice she couldn't control.

He grinned at her with pure male satisfaction. "Are you ready for more?"

She liked the new playfulness between them. "Bring it on, big boy."

His grin only widened. "Simon says bring that pussy up here."

She gave him a questioning look. "You want me to—"

He cut her off by the simple expedient of grabbing her hips and lifting her over his chest. Damn, that man was strong.

"Lean up on your knees, baby. Give me your pussy. Right over my mouth."

"You're serious?" They'd never done this before. In fact, she'd never done it in this position with anyone, ever.

"Oh yeah." He gave her a mischievous wink. "I want a taste of you, baby. I want to fuck you with my tongue and have your cream dribble down my chin."

Her abdomen clenched at his earthy words and she responded to the urging of his hands, rising above him into the position he desired. She wasn't sure about this, but the hidden temptress within wanted—no, needed—to do anything he asked. His dirty talk affected her more than she would have believed possible. If any other man had used such language with her, she wasn't sure she could have responded. Coming from Simon's lips? Those words were thrilling in a forbidden, very naughty way. He made her feel sexy, desired, and almost…wanton. Only for him.

A moment later, his mouth rose to her core, his tongue exploring, licking through her folds and right up into her. He set a rhythm that made her groan, stabbing into her over and over again with his tongue in an imitation of what he would do later with his cock, if she had her way.

She couldn't hold it. Not one second longer. She shattered with a shaking moan as she came against his tongue. He made a sound that vibrated against her most sensitive parts, drawing out her hasty orgasm. After a minute or two, it plateaued, but didn't fully dissipate. If their past history was anything to go by, she was in for one hell of a ride. He'd done this to her a few times before—brought her multiple orgasms, each one building on the last until she flew right up to the stars.

Simon was, by far, the most talented lover she had ever had the good fortune to be with. This was especially true when he took his time…and they had the day all to themselves. She shuddered just thinking of what he could do in that time.

When he came up for air, she was finally able to move away. He wouldn't let her go far. He parked her over his chest, sitting lightly on her haunches, her legs spread for him, her core displayed for him to look at. And play with.

His hands stroked from her hips to her pussy with tantalizing slowness. He watched her face, searching her reaction, then slid his gaze to her spread folds with heated intensity. That look alone was enough to make her cream.

"Spread your legs a little farther for me, baby, and lean back. I want to see all of you."

She felt very vulnerable, spread out and open to him. She wouldn't have done this for just anyone. This was Simon. He could have anything he asked of her. He was her savior, her protector, the only man she had ever loved. If she could bear to make herself vulnerable to any man, it was him. She complied, the straining muscles of her thighs shaking as she moved into the position he wanted.

One of his big hands spread her open even farther. Then a broad, male finger slid into her channel, making her gasp. He set up a rhythm that picked up on her earlier climax and drove her passion higher. He didn't let the pleasure dissipate. No, he kept her primed while he inspected her pussy, adding a second finger after a while that made her squirm in earnest. Then his thumb started to tease her clit and all hell broke loose. Again.

"Simon!" She cried out as she peaked again and heard him chuckle. That masculine sound drove her higher. It told her he was enjoying making her squeal with pleasure and come for him.

She came on his hand, moaning as she shook with satisfaction. It rose in a tide and never receded. He was definitely working her toward something bigger and better. She only hoped she would still be able to breathe when he finally got her to the destination he had in mind.

Mariana gave over all control to him willingly and followed where he led. She knew enough about him to know he would make it worth her while. If there was one thing she knew Simon wanted, it was her trust. She had trusted him with her life already. Now she would trust him again, this time with her body and her pleasure. She knew she couldn't be in better hands.

When the shudders began to subside, he removed his fingers. His hands stroked over her skin, cupping her breasts and teasing the sensitive nipples, then lingering over her ticklish abdomen and down into her wet, eager, wide open pussy. He didn't give her time to come down off the climax; instead, he built her toward another.

"Are you up for more, baby?"

She nodded, entranced by the glittering need in his sexy

blue eyes.

"What would you say if Simon said to suck my cock?" His words dared her to be wanton and she responded in kind.

"I'd say, what took you so long?" The smile she gave him was full of feminine mischief and sloe-eyed audaciousness. Her inner siren had come out to play.

Her body craved the small respite and her mind wanted to even the score with her sexy tormentor. She wanted to bring him along with her on their path to ecstasy. She didn't like for it all to be one sided, with him giving her everything and her selfishly taking it all. She wanted to give to him, too.

"Then Simon says, give it your all, baby. Suck it down but don't make me come. I want to come inside you."

"I live to follow your orders," she teased with a roll of her eyes as she levered herself off his muscular body. For this, she wanted to be at his side, able to devote her entire attention to doing him right. He deserved no less after the two brilliant peaks he'd already given her.

She licked the head, teasing at first, watching his reactions to check his responses. Hooded eyes followed her every move. She liked the power he gave her over his pleasure. It made her feel more in control and supremely feminine. Just what she needed after her feeling of helplessness leftover from the dream—a little give and take. He owned her pleasure but he'd given her some control over his.

Wanting more, she opened her mouth wide and took him in. She loved the sexy groan that issued from his lips when she hollowed her cheeks and applied suction.

"Oh, baby, just like that," he praised, clenching his hands into fists at his sides, rumpling the sheets in his hands. The way the sleek muscles of his washboard abdomen rippled sent shivers down her spine. He really was the sexiest man alive. And he was all hers. A girl couldn't get any luckier than this.

She grabbed the root of him with one hand and squeezed, fondling his sac gently with the other. His grunts and groans were music to her ears as she applied herself to making him come. He'd told her not to push him that far, but she remembered his powers of recovery and amazing stamina. She knew it wouldn't take him long to make a comeback even after she had drained him dry. He wouldn't leave her hanging, and if she let him, he would give and give and never take even this small thing for himself.

She loved him for it, but he had to learn that sometimes she wanted to be the one giving in their relationship, not just the recipient of his amazing talents. She sucked him long and strong, gauging his reactions with increasing pleasure. He tried to pull away once. She held firm and wouldn't let him leave. Truth be told, he didn't put up that much of a struggle and she figured she'd won this round. Feminine satisfaction filled her with a giddy sort of triumph and she redoubled her efforts.

Mariana knew darn well how much he liked what she was doing to him. Inwardly she purred, knowing the sound would travel as vibrations down his sensitive length. He groaned her name as he came. He tried to pull away again, but she wouldn't let him escape. She wanted everything he had to give.

It had been so long. She remembered his taste, the unique saltiness of him. Of the few men she'd done this to in her life, Simon was the only man who made her truly yearn for the taste of him. He was her perfect match in every way.

His breath came in great gasps and his eyes were squeezed tightly shut as she watched him come down from his explosive orgasm.

"You're a witch, Mari. A siren sent to seduce me. And you're a little cheater. I told you not to do that." His eyes popped open to find her, still sitting at his side, trailing lazy fingers over his rippled abdomen.

"Come on, Simon. You know you liked it." She smiled slyly at him, encouraging him to admit his delight.

"Oh, I liked it all right." He lifted up on one elbow to meet her gaze. "But it's not what I told you to do. You disobeyed a direct order, woman." The teasing tone of his voice reassured her that he wasn't really mad at her. He was, however, in a playful mood, which could mean a lot of different things. Simon had always been an inventive lover. She couldn't wait to see what he would pull out of his bag of tricks now.

"It was in a good cause, sir." She gave a sloppy salute as a grin split her lips.

"I won't argue that, Doctor. However, when Simon says to do something, in future you need to learn that he means it."

"Really?" One of her eyebrows rose in challenge.

"Really." She knew from the way he answered that he was amused by their banter. "I ought to swat your ass for disobeying me."

"Would you, really?" Damn, was that breathy, porn star voice really hers?

Okay, so maybe the idea of a sexy spanking had run through her mind a few times, but she had never let anyone actually do it to her. She had never given up that kind of control to anyone. Of course, she'd never done a lot of the things Simon had introduced her to and she had loved every one of them. If there was anyone on Earth she could trust, Simon was the guy she could trust to explore all her forbidden fantasies. She was safe with him. He would never hurt her and he would listen and obey if she said she wanted to stop.

"Is that anticipation I hear?" She saw his cock stir as one of his hands trailed down from her waist to her backside, cupping one rounded cheek. As she'd thought, it didn't take long for him to rise to the occasion once more. The man was fit and had stamina to spare. That was a good thing in a warrior—and especially in a lover.

His fingers tightened on her ass, then let go, only to come back in a stinging smack that made her jump. A high pitched squeal came from her lips that she hadn't expected. Neither had she expected the slight burn of her flesh that made her want more.

Oh, yeah. Simon knew her all too well if that one swat was

any indication. She wanted more.

"Well?" Blue eyes dared her as he sat up fully, facing her.

She blinked up at him and purred playfully. "Please sir, may I have another?"

Simon laughed outright and she loved the sound. He did it so rarely outside of their time together, it was a gift.

"Just for that, wench..." He lifted her as if she weighed nothing at all and scooted to the edge of the bed. In an eye blink, she was draped over his knees, ass in the air. "You're gonna get it."

"Oh, I hope so." She squealed again when his hand came down in a playful swat.

He didn't really hurt her, just smacked her hard enough for a delicious burn to spread over her skin. And the way her rubbed her cheeks with that big, open palm before and after the light taps was even more rewarding than the naughty feeling being spanked gave her.

It wasn't something she would like to do every night, but as a change of pace, it certainly had its rewards. She had never been all that daring sexually. Not until Simon. He'd given her everything she had ever fantasized about and more. He seemed to know what she wanted even before she did and he always put her pleasure first. Nothing, it seemed, was too much to ask.

Which was why she let him lead in the bedroom. This was a man who didn't need an instruction manual to find his way around a woman's body. No, Simon had probably *written* the damned manual.

In all, he spent more time stroking her skin than actually spanking her. He took his time, letting his fingers stray downward, between her legs, to linger and tease. When she squirmed, so near the edge, he startled her back away from it with another little tap. He repeated this process a few times until she couldn't control the moans that issued from her lips or the shivery sensations coursing through her body. She needed to come. Bad. And he had to know it.

"So responsive, my dear," he mused as he cupped her

stinging cheek with one big hand. "We'll have to remember this for the future. Maybe someday you can play naughty schoolgirl for me."

Just thinking about the scene his words implied made her thighs clench. She was so close!

"Ah, I see you like the idea. I didn't know you were quite so kinky, Mari, but it's a pleasure to find out. I'll play any game you like. Anytime." He leaned over to growl the last bit in her ear and she couldn't help the shivers that went down her spine, straight to her pussy.

"Simon! Please," she gasped, wanting him. Waiting for him to push her over the edge again.

His hand came down in one final swat and she cried out, coming hard. She wouldn't have thought she could gain such satisfaction from being spanked, but Simon had always been able to pull things out of her response she never would have expected.

"Now, are you going to disobey me ever again?" She heard the laughter in his voice as he leaned over her.

"Every chance I get," she whispered, still coming down from a blissful place.

"Hmm. Maybe I ought to rethink my strategy." He rubbed her ass one final time and lifted her to lie on her back in the center of the bed as she laughed with him.

It was good to feel so carefree after the tense days they'd just spent. Especially after the months spent apart, months she had spent missing him.

"Come to me, Simon." She cupped his cheek as he laid her down, her gaze holding his. "Make love to me."

He stilled over her. "Who's giving the orders here?" The words were playful, but his tone wasn't. No, he'd gone serious on her, mirroring her mood and turning the needful moment into something much more serious.

"I need you, Simon. I've always needed you."

Silence stretched. She had to dare. She had to give him what she thought he finally might truly want.

"I love you, Simon. I never stopped loving you."

His reaction didn't show on his face, but she saw satisfaction and relief in his expression as he moved over her. Without a word, he joined with her, sliding into her body and claiming her for his own. At least, that's what it felt like. He began to move in a slow, steady rhythm that she matched eagerly.

Something big was happening here. It was different than it ever had been before. The urgency was there, but ratcheted back to let the emotion pour over and through. She felt all the things she always felt when Simon was inside her— protected, cherished, cared for in a deep, lingering way. She felt something else as well, moving deeply between them, in the space of their souls.

Her words of love had affected him. She felt it in every deep stroke, every moment he held her gaze. Nothing stood between them now. Raw emotion touched his face and she knew he saw the same from her.

"I have only one more thing I want you to do, baby." He kept his steady pace, drawing out the moment.

"What's that?" Her voice was breathless.

"Simon says, marry me?"

A laugh started from her lips as she reached up to encircle his neck.

"Yes, Simon. Oh, yes!"

He kissed her then, joining their bodies in every possible way as his strokes increased. He was wild at the last, holding her by the shoulders so his hard thrusts didn't push her up against the headboard. She was cocooned by him, surrounded and engulfed by him, and it felt wonderful.

They came together in a shower of passionate sparks that set them both aflame with rapture, flying higher than ever before. Together. Forever.

If fate allowed.

What felt like hours later, Mariana woke. Simon lay beside her, propped up on one elbow watching her.

"Did I fall asleep?"

"I think you passed out." He grinned. "I'm sorry, honey. I didn't mean to push you so hard. Are you okay?"

She stretched sore limbs, taking stock. "I'm glorious."

"That you are, my love." One big hand stroked her rib cage, tracing delicate patterns on her skin.

"Did you mean it, Simon? Do you really want to get married?"

"Yes, Mari. I know it's selfish, but I need you. I can't live without you. I…love you." His expression looked pained for a split second. "I've never said that to a woman before. I've never felt it before, but I feel it with you, Mari. I've loved you for a long time. In fact…" He reached over the side of the bed and fished something out of the pocket of his pants, then threw them aside once more. "I bought this a while back, with the intention of giving it to you when I returned from that last mission. Then things happened, and well, now you know the rest. The thing is, I never could put this away. I've carried it all this time and now I know why."

He held out his hand and opened his fist, palm up. On it sparkled a diamond ring that took her breath away.

"This is yours, Mari. I bought it for you. Will you accept it? Will you accept me, knowing what happened to me? Knowing there's a heap of uncertainty in my life and about my future? Knowing that I love you and want to spend whatever time I have left with you? Knowing that I've loved you since we first met and it's taken me all this time to find the courage to tell you?"

"Oh, Simon." She sat up, tears in her eyes as she reached for his hand. He captured hers and placed the ring on her finger himself. The moment seemed sacred, somehow.

"I love you, Mariana, and I always will."

"I love you, Simon. No matter what comes, we'll be together." Tears rolled down her face as he kissed her, cementing their love.

They'd have a ceremony later and a big party with their friends and family, but all that really mattered was their love. Undying, unable to be destroyed by time, distance, or horror.

They had each other now, and that was all that mattered. Or so Simon said.

#

ABOUT THE AUTHOR

Bianca D'Arc has run a laboratory, climbed the corporate ladder in the shark-infested streets of lower Manhattan, studied and taught martial arts, and earned the right to put a whole bunch of letters after her name, but she's always enjoyed writing more than any of her other pursuits. She grew up and still lives on Long Island, where she keeps busy with an extensive garden, several aquariums full of very demanding fish, and writing her favorite genres of paranormal, fantasy and sci-fi romance.

Bianca loves to hear from readers and can be reached through Twitter (@BiancaDArc), Facebook (BiancaDArcAuthor) or through the various links on her website.

WELCOME TO THE D'ARC SIDE…
WWW.BIANCADARC.COM

OTHER BOOKS BY BIANCA D'ARC

Brotherhood of Blood
One & Only
Rare Vintage
Phantom Desires
Sweeter Than Wine
Forever Valentine
Wolf Hills*
Wolf Quest

Tales of the Were
Lords of the Were
Inferno

Tales of the Were ~
The Others
Rocky
Slade

Tales of the Were ~
String of Fate
Cat's Cradle
King's Throne
Jacob's Ladder
Her Warriors

Tales of the Were ~
Redstone Clan
The Purrfect Stranger
Grif
Red
Magnus
Bobcat
Matt

Tales of the Were ~
Grizzly Cove
All About the Bear
Mating Dance
Night Shift
Alpha Bear
Saving Grace
Bearliest Catch
The Bear's Healing Touch
The Luck of the Shifters
Badass Bear

Tales of the Were ~
Were-Fey Love Story
Lone Wolf
Snow Magic
Midnight Kiss

Tales of the Were ~
Jaguar Island (Howls)
The Jaguar Tycoon
The Jaguar Bodyguard

Gemini Project
Tag Team
Doubling Down

Resonance Mates
Hara's Legacy**
Davin's Quest
Jaci's Experiment
Grady's Awakening
Harry's Sacrifice

Dragon Knights

Daughters of the Dragon
Maiden Flight*
Border Lair
The Ice Dragon**
Prince of Spies***

Dragon Knights ~ Novellas
The Dragon Healer
Master at Arms
Wings of Change

Sons of Draconia
FireDrake
Dragon Storm
Keeper of the Flame
Hidden Dragons

The Sea Captain's Daughter
Book 1: Sea Dragon
Book 2: Dragon Fire
Book 3: Dragon Mates

Guardians of the Dark
Half Past Dead
Once Bitten, Twice Dead
A Darker Shade of Dead
The Beast Within
Dead Alert

StarLords
Hidden Talent
Talent For Trouble
Shy Talent

Jit'Suku Chronicles ~ Arcana
King of Swords
King of Cups
King of Clubs
King of Stars
End of the Line
Diva

Jit'Suku Chronicles ~ Sons of Amber
Angel in the Badlands
Master of Her Heart

StarLords
Hidden Talent
Talent For Trouble
Shy Talent

Gifts of the Ancients
Warrior's Heart

* RT Book Reviews Awards Nominee
** EPPIE Award Winner
*** CAPA Award Winner

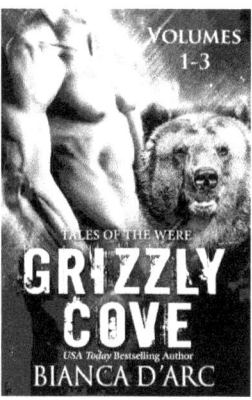

The first three Grizzly Cove stories in one place!

Welcome to Grizzly Cove, where bear shifters can be who they are - if the creatures of the deep will just leave them be. Wild magic, unexpected allies, a conflagration of sorcery and shifter magic the likes of which has not been seen in centuries... That's what awaits the peaceful town of Grizzly Cove. That, and love. Lots and lots of love.

This anthology contains:

All About the Bear
Welcome to Grizzly Cove, where the sheriff has more than the peace to protect. The proprietor of the new bakery in town is clueless about the dual nature of her nearest neighbors, but not for long. It'll be up to Sheriff Brody to clue her in and convince her to stay calm—and in his bed—for the next fifty years or so.

Mating Dance
Tom, Grizzly Cove's only lawyer, is also a badass grizzly bear, but he's met his match in Ashley, the woman he just can't get out of his mind. She's got a dark secret, that only he knows. When ugliness from her past tracks her to her new home, can Tom protect the woman he is fast coming to believe is his mate?

Night Shift
Sheriff's Deputy Zak is one of the few black bear shifters in a colony of grizzlies. When his job takes him into closer proximity to the lovely Tina, though, he finds he can't resist her. Could it be he's finally found his mate? And when adversity strikes, will she turn to him, or run into the night? Zak will do all he can to make sure she chooses him.

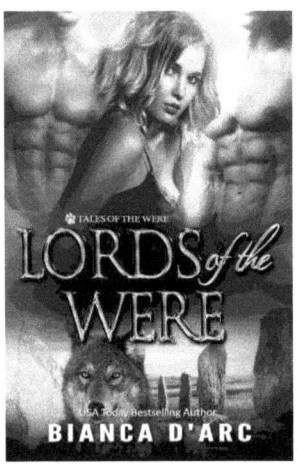

Allie is about to discover a heritage of power…and blood…werecreatures, magic, and a misguided vampire who wants to kill two men who could be the loves of her life.

Allie was adopted. She had always known it, but when a mysterious older woman shows up and invites her to learn about her birth family, things take a turn for the odd.

Then Allie meets the Lords. Twin Alpha werewolves who rule over all North American were, Rafe and Tim may look exactly alike, but Allie can tell them apart from the moment they first meet. She's not sure what to think when they both want to claim her as their mate.

They are dominant, sexy, and all too ready to play games of the most delicious kind with her, but when a rogue vampire threatens her safety, they jump to her defense. It will take all of them working together, to stop the evil that has invaded their territory. Can they trust in each other and the power of their new love to prevail? Or will an ancient enemy win the day and usher evil incarnate back into the world?

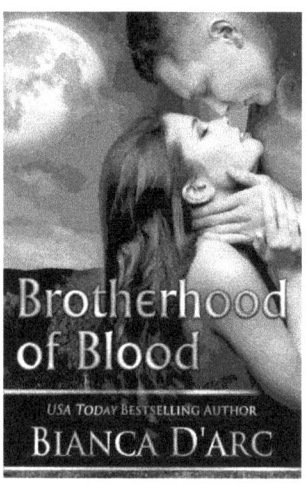

The first three novellas in the critically acclaimed vampire romance series, now in one place...

One & Only
Atticus is about to give up and greet the sun when he finds the love of his eternal life...by accident.

Rare Vintage
Marc, Master vampire of the Napa Valley, can't keep away from Kelly, no matter how many sparks fly between them. When an enemy challenges his authority, will she sacrifice her life for his?

Phantom Desires
Master Dmitri's lair is located under a farmhouse in rural Wyoming. Spying on the new owner while she sleeps could be more dangerous than even he suspects.

WWW.BIANCADARC.COM

Lightning Source UK Ltd.
Milton Keynes UK
UKHW011846041119
352881UK00019B/415/P